A Healthy Fear

By

Rhonda Boothe

First paperback edition Sept 2024

Book editing by Zephanasia Lewis

Book design by Immaculate Studios

Registration Number: TXu 2-409-734

Meet The Author

Rhonda Boothe is a creative soul born in the West End of Henrico County, just outside Richmond Virginia. During the 1980's, I grew up in a community much like Heritage Park in this story. Life for me growing up with my parents and two brothers was amazing. I could not have asked for a more balanced and beautiful upbringing. So many people, experiences, and moments helped shape this story and the woman I am today. I never dreamed I would be an aspiring writer when I graduated high school in 1996. I immediately attended college and during this time is when I began to realize I had a knack for writing. Term papers and writing assignments were much easier for me than tests. I graduated from Christopher Newport University with a degree in Biology and worked in that field, mostly doing quality food analysis for more than a decade. I grew tired of that industry and completely switched gears after taking a personality test. The results showed that I should be in sales, and I did just that. At the age of 34, diving into the world of commission-based sales with no safety net was a huge change for me. I wasn't any good at first, but after about a year of dedication and hard work, I began to flourish in that role.

Sometime around 2015, I started to develop the story for "A Healthy Fear". I had a recent heartfelt conversation with a former coworker about his past abuse and in that moment, all those similar conversations I had with various people over the years just parked themselves in my brain. It was heartbreaking to know that so many people around me were living with such deep past traumas and considered me a sort of therapist. For many years after, something in my soul told me to write about it. I convinced myself that I wasn't a writer and just continued to immerse myself in my sales career. In 2021, I suffered the loss of my mom, which left me completely devastated. I felt as though life was closing in on me and I had nothing to lose anymore. This point in time led me to start the process of getting this story out of my head and onto paper. I began to passively outline characters and storylines while continuing to work my sales job. In early 2023, I had routine surgery and was out of work for 8 weeks. To keep myself busy, I started to construct "A Healthy Fear". It eventually took me a year to complete, but I felt so accomplished when I was done. So many of my close friends and family read my story as it developed and cheered me on. My village is amazing and encouraged me every step of the way. I currently live a quiet, simple life in the city of Richmond. I enjoy writing, walking my dogs, and spending time with family and friends. I have two more books in the works, so stay tuned!

"A Healthy Fear" is completely fiction and in no way reflects the actual events experienced by those who confided in me. All characters and events are made up though they may exist as a reality for many. I hope this book touches lives, ignites change for victims, and sparks conversations for readers. Thank you for taking the time to read my book!

To those who matter:

First and foremost, this book is dedicated to Willie and Mary Boothe. You have no idea how grateful I am to have had you both as parents growing up. You loved me, you protected me, you nurtured me, but most of all, YOU INSPIRED ME! I think of you every day. Until I see your beautiful faces again, I LOVE YOU!

Alannah: I am humbled by the presence of your intelligence. Thank you for allowing me to bug you at all hours of the day with ideas. Thank you for being the voice of reason and sound decisions throughout this process. It's only up from here, I LOVE YOU!

Charnise: A person can only be so lucky to have a best friend like you. Over 30 years of love and patience, I know I can be a bit much at times. You are my biggest cheerleader and have provided me with so much positive feedback while writing this book. Once I get my seat at the table, you will be right there with me, I LOVE YOU!

I can't name everybody, but there are a host of friends and family who have supported me throughout this process. You know who you are. I will continue to make you all proud, I LOVE YOU!

I must acknowledge the person who first gave me the idea to present this manuscript to the world as a book. I was determined to pitch it as a movie, but you told me to do the book first, a movie will come. THANK YOU BINKY, best idea ever!

TABLE OF CONTENTS

CHAPTER 1

DAN "THE MAN"

Coach Dan scans the football field as summer begins to make its way into Heritage Park, Virginia. He is looking at upcoming freshman hopefuls who are trying out to replace the large number of outgoing senior football players, most of which are now college freshman themselves. There is much pressure from the community to repeat Heritage Park High's past glory, successfully led by Coach Dan Butler. "All goddamn trash," Dan barks to his assistant, Rick, as he slams a clipboard full of papers to the ground. Dan drops his head in frustration as the practice squad assembles on the field. The school year is coming to an end, but football is year-round at Heritage Park High. It is the summer of 1987, and Heritage Park, the outlining suburb of the very urban and more densely populated city of Ridgeland, is beginning to become a big deal as it is experiencing its own population increase and growth unlike anything it has never seen before. This is mainly due to the influx of newly settled Black residents spilling over from the Ridgeland city limits. Re-zoning and integration have made way for this once sleepy town to grow. Industry sprouting everywhere as the vast land, once used for farming and hunting, is now a bustling landscape. Constant construction makes way for carefully carved out subdivisions, apartment complexes, and industrial parks. Production plants also add to the population explosion in Heritage Park. White collar businessmen breathing new life into the area. Heritage Park is growing, and everyone is excited and welcoming. Coach Dan is at the center of it all!

Coach Dan Butler has successfully led the Heritage Park Tigers to seven championships over the last eleven years; he has won six. He has also sent dozens of high school seniors to prestigious college football programs all over the United States. Dan, also affectionately known as "Dan the man" throughout the community, is well known and well connected, due to his illustrious football program. Dan has neatly combed light brown hair with a few wispy grays at the sideburns. His hair is neatly tucked under his coach's hat to catch the sweat brought on by the unrelenting Virginia sun. He stands about five feet, - nine inches, one hundred and eighty fit pounds. His posture is admirable as he is a much more imposing figure in person than on paper. His skin is a peachy shade of white with a reddish olive tint, a product of his ample time spent in the sun and his Greek lineage on his mother's side. Now, in his late forties, everyone comments on how good he looks for his age. Dan wears the same neatly pressed style of outfit every day during the summer months. A long-collared polyester knit, four-button shirt, and a pair of nylon blend, sharply creased shorts that extended almost to his knees. Always the same pairings, only varying colors. Dan is charismatic, sometimes funny, but mostly stoic as he takes his overachieving football team and beautiful family very seriously.

No drinking, no drugs, and no smoking at a time when all were socially acceptable. Dan opted not to indulge and expects the same from his family and players. Dan is married to Mary Butler, a short, beautiful, demure blonde who is widely considered the epitome of grace and class. Always in a dress with tights and always displayed in a perfectly presented package. She appears like a forty-year-old debutant at every public outing. The two have been a couple since childhood it seems. No one can recall either of them having ever been in any other relationship; they have just always seemed to be together. Mary has never worked, though, she holds a college degree in education herself. Her only job is to meticulously maintain the house for Dan and their two kids. Sarah, nineteen, and Michael, twenty-one, are both away at different colleges. Arguably the most well-mannered and best-looking kids in the whole town of Heritage Park. Tall, lean, athletic, intellectual, both play sports, and maintain very high GPAs, an expectation in the Butler household. "Yes sir" and "Yes ma'am" are commonly heard when in their presence, and Dan wouldn't have it any other way. Dan and his family are the quintessential, textbook standard of what every white American family strived to be.

Dan was born and raised in Heritage Park and has remained there his whole life, other than the four years he spent away at college. He graduated from state university in 1962, moved back home, and has been a prominent fixture ever since. Dan has been a part of the local high school in some capacity or another over the last twenty years, the head coach for the last eleven years. If you know anything about Heritage Park, you know the name "Butler." Everyone knows the Butler family for one reason or another. Arrogance is an understatement as it pertains to Dan Butler. He holds intimate secrets of many of the who's who in Heritage Park, many of the longtime residents remain at the top of a fictitious social hierarchy within the community. He has never been afraid to speak openly and candidly regarding the affairs of others when he needs leverage in matters of disagreement. He has a sharp tongue and thinks little of the fall out and dismay he leaves behind in the shadow of his cruelty. He once asked a local store owner if he needed to borrow more money in front of his wife and kids, all because the gentleman asked Dan about a game loss decision. He is also said to have once spit on a gardener who he felt destroyed a highly visible shrub in his meticulously maintained front yard. Almost everyone in the community has directly experienced or heard a story of Coach Dan's wrath. He is "no nonsense" in his approach to friends, family, players, colleagues, and business associates. He must have control of all people in his life. Dan himself jokingly remarks often that everyone in the community should have a "healthy fear" of him.

CHAPTER 2

"PROSPECTING WOES"

The summer always brings in a new batch of athletic hopefuls. This year is no different, except the prospect pool looks miserable, and Dan is none too happy. Flat foot and out of shape, there are at least thirty young candidates waiting for the opportunity to play for the state champion Tigers. "This can't be it!" Dan's tone loud and aggressive as he speaks to Rick, his assistant coach. "Have you scouted all of the incoming freshmen and new student rosters?" Rick replies, "Of course. I'm as frustrated as you Dan. I just don't get it." "How do we make a team out of this shit? We only have three months until pre-season scrimmages. I NEED PLAYERS!" Dan's voice elevates; a few nearby students hear him. "I could lose my job for this bullshit," says Dan. Rick calmly replies, "Nonsense, you're talking crazy now. We'll figure something out, even if we just whip what we got into shape. Work 'em to death this summer. No breaks. Plus, we still have four or five solid upcoming seniors left over from last year's team. Let's just build the team around them." Defeat in his tone, Dan replies, "I don't think it's enough. Plus, we need a quarterback. Hell, I need a star dammit!" Rick confidently assures Dan, "We have time. I will make sure we put something together, even if I gotta snag a few homeboys from the city and let 'em use my address." The two share a brief chuckle as they walk onto the field and order the players to divide into two lines, preparing for a passing drill.

Coach Rick, Dan's assistant, is a compact, dumpy little man, standing only about five feet, six inches on his tiptoes. He maintains the perfect balance of fat and muscle on his squatty, yet stocky, frame. His clothes are never neatly pressed and rarely fit properly. His sneakers are always run-down but seem to allow him optimal movement as he coaches the kids. Rick is anywhere between twenty-nine and thirty-nine years old. It's more of a mystery as he has never revealed his age or birthday to anyone in town. He has a very racially ambiguous appearance. Big black, thick, silky curls wildly cover his entire head, and it seems like he will never go bald. With a light tan complexion and hazel eyes, he could be Hispanic, mixed race (black and white), or even a mix of every race of which you can think. He tells everyone he is of Cherokee descent, which is believable given his appearance. No one knows and no one cares, as no one has ever seen anyone from his family.

He has no kids or wife to speak of. Some people find it odd, but at this point, he is a fixture in the community and can usually be found trotting behind Dan on the football field. He presents as a kind of flunky. He all but begged to be a part of the football program at Heritage Park. Dan finally relented after two years of pretty much torturing him with work for the team, without pay. Rick loves to smoke and drink when he gets a chance, which is the main reason it took Dan so long to add him to the program. Over time, Dan felt the level of dedication outweighed his bad habits. No one really knows where Rick came from, why he came, or what his game plan is, but after three years in, everyone in the community has just learned to accept him as Coach Dan's faithful assistant.

Dan and Rick are overlooking the practice squads as they run the passing drills instructed by Rick earlier. It's so bad that Dan can't bear to look. Some of the passes barely make it to the intended partner. Not one tight spiral in sight, all wabbly and weak as they are released from the delicate little hands of the perspective players. Beyond defeated, Dan blows his whistle to end practice early. It is only 5:00 p.m., but Dan has seen enough. He yells out to the boys, "Hit the showers, and get ready to be grinded to a nub tomorrow. I mean it!" As the boys run off the field, frolicking in delight to be done with practice early, Rick and Dan flop on bleachers in disbelief. "Where are the blacks I normally have?" barks Dan at Rick. Rick gestures for Dan to keep it down as there are some students lingering around the field from the outdoor track team. Dan lowers his tone a bit, "The white players just don't have the same athletic ability." Rick responds in a whisper, "I know we have had success with the Black players as the lead and a few solid whites as supporting cast. We may have to switch it up a bit this year. Whip the ones we have into shape and work with the leftovers from last year." Dan agrees but tells Rick that he may need to take him up on that plan from earlier. Dan says in a low whisper, "I know we've never done this before, but instead of waiting for the Black people to come to us, we may need to recruit in the city, and use some of the boosters' addresses. I know it's dishonest, but I'm getting desperate!" With skepticism in his voice, Rick responds, "Oh Dan, that's bad news. There's nothing good that can come of that if it gets out. I was honestly joking earlier." Thinking of the potential scandal that would ensue, Dan agrees, "You're right; the whole town would turn on me. I can't risk it."

Rick reassures Dan, "It's too early to panic; we still have all summer, and I feel confident something good is going to happen!" Dan replies, "Damn Ricky, I sure hope you're right. I'm not a religious man, but I sure think I'm going to go home and pray about it." The two men arise from the bleachers. Dan heads for the parking lot, and Rick heads to the gym to wait for the players to leave so he can lock up.

CHAPTER 3

"UNEXPECTED BOUNTY"

Coach Dan was once both teacher and football coach earlier in his career. He is a known history buff and unintentionally impresses people when he rattles off early American historical facts. Due to his vast knowledge and degree in American History, he was, at one time, excited to teach students about the past of this great nation he held in such high regard. But as time wore on and the football program grew, in true Dan fashion, he pretty much said he wasn't going to do both anymore. The school board initially fought him on the decision, as they would now have to meet his new salary demands and hire a teacher to take his place. Met with this opposition, Dan threatened to leave altogether without batting an eye. The school board knew this would cause very bad blood within the community and could ruin their chances of obtaining additional funding they needed from the state. They reluctantly relented and gave Dan his way, as he knew they would. Dan was also able to secure a small stipend for Rick as well. So now, even though he is no longer a teacher, he has access to everything the teachers do, receives a full salary for teaching and an additional salary for coaching. Dan also has an office bigger than all the administrators in the school, including the principal.

All the students love and respect Dan, even though he typically pays them no mind and ignores much of what they say in passing. During school hours, you can find him sitting in his office reading sports publications, organizing scouting reports and play books with Rick, or in his personal bathroom, his favorite place of all. It is no secret that Rick does most of the heavy lifting in this partnership. Dan just kind of gets all the recognition, and Rick is just fine with this; he seems to get joy out of simply being included. On this particular day, at the tail end of May, Dan is in his office preparing for practice in three hours.

He is diligently writing down the murderous drills he is planning for the players later. He promised them torture, and he intends to do just that! One of his fellow administrators pops her head in to remind Dan that the school board is having a meeting this coming Friday and his attendance is mandatory! Marcy, the administrative office manager, who is a short, shapeless woman with a very homely appearance that Dan loathes. Dan views Marcy as unrefined white trash, a disgrace to decent white folks. She has dyed dark brown hair, teased bangs, stiff as metal wire, and a shoulder length bob hairstyle that is about twenty years outdated.

Marcy casually leans in the doorway of Dan's office and starts speaking without a formal greeting or any warning. "Hey hon, don't forget about the school board meeting this Friday. We need you there this time; we need to chat about the school budget." She stares, waiting for Dan to reply in the affirmative while aggressively chewing and popping bubble gum. Dan's face immediately displays annoyance at the audacity of her interrupting his task as well as her insistence that he MUST do anything! Her appearance, her callous tone in broken English, and the loud gum chewing was all too much. Dan is known to be very harsh and swift with his tongue, and given the situation, this was about to be one of those moments. Without even giving her the opportunity to say another word, Dan blurts out, "Marcy, aren't you married? I think I recall you have a husband, correct?" Marcy stares at Dan, baffled by such an odd, off-subject question. "Of course, Dan. You met my husband, Jim, many times. What does that have to do with anything?" "Oh nothing." Dan appears nonchalant, though, seething on the inside. "It's just that I thought I saw you and Mr. Barnes, the tennis coach, in your car a couple of weeks ago. I was leaving a late practice when saw what I didn't think I was seeing. Back parking lot. Hell, it must've been nine o'clock. My eyes aren't the best, though; maybe I have it all wrong." Marcy's face turns beet red as her eyes begin to swell with tears. Embarrassed at what she obviously hadn't thought anyone saw. She immediately turns and swiftly exits Dan's office. A sense of self-gratification showers over Dan, as he feels accomplished for a job well done! "I bet that'll teach you, bitch!" Dan scoffs and continues with the task he was doing before Marcy rudely interrupted.

There is no doubt that Dan never physically laid eyes on Marcy in the back parking lot with anyone. But he has a small, dedicated group of snitches at school and around town in general. They have an unwavering dedication to staying in his good graces by any means. Rick is undoubtedly Dan's top tattle tell. He is most likely the source of the information Dan just relayed to Marcy as he is often on the school grounds late. He quietly sees and hears everything and consistently reports his findings to Dan immediately. Dan usually takes in the information brought to him and just holds on to it until he needs it, much like in the situation just displayed with Marcy.

Dan heads to the field with his notes prepared for the upcoming torture session he has lined up. There is a level of excitement for this practice, as Dan feels like the recruits are weak and need to be broken, as athletes and as individuals. He looks over the crowd of about thirty students in disgust. Lazy and unaware of what they are about to endure, they playfully laugh and crack jokes at one another. If they make it through this practice and return tomorrow, Dan will most likely view them as high potential prospects for the upcoming season. Dan's attention is diverted as Rick comes darting across the field. Disheveled and sloppy, not far from the way he normally looks, he posts up next to Dan, completely out of breath. "What did I miss?" Rick whispers to Dan. He is about to give Rick a very snide reply but thinks better, as he has bigger fish to fry. He silently gives Rick about seven seconds worth of a death stare directly into his eyes, then turns and refocuses on the assembled students.

Dan blows his whistle with enough force to get the attention of everyone on the field, off the field, in the parking lot, and beyond. Even Rick is startled by the deafening sound. The boys immediately straighten up and focus on both coaches. Dan yells with a thunderous tone, "All of you, drop and do fifty push-ups. If I see you cheating or lying down, you will start over. Immediately after those, we are doing one hundred burpee drills. After that, you will do fifty-forty (sprint to the forty-yard line and back twenty-five times). Then you will run a mile on the track, and I expect your time to be less than nine minutes. If you do not come in under nine minutes, you will run until you do. I don't care if it's ten o'clock at night. Rick will make sure you stay until you're done." Rick sharply snaps his bushy hair towards Dan and looks as if he is caught off guard by the statement. The boys all drop in unison and immediately start their push-ups. Dan has already set up the cones for the drills at various stations on the field. He orders Rick to go over and closely supervise the drills.

Dan steps back so he can inspect their form and spot any impassioned fortitude out of the bunch. While doing so, Dan catches something out of the corner of his eye. He diverts his attention away from the drills to witness what must've been the most beautiful sight Dan has seen all year! A tightly thrown, spiraled football pass thrown for what seems to be almost thirty yards. The intended target is a medium height, clumsy, unkept Black kid, who drops the perfect pass as if he weren't even trying to catch it. He retrieves the football, and steps in several feet, understanding his range is different from the other boy's. The weaker boy heaves the football with all his might in the direction of the stronger of the two boys. Awkward and wobbly in the air, the stronger boy adjusts to the pass and ends up effortlessly catching the football with just one hand. This has Dan's attention as he watches closely behind his mirror-tinted aviator shades. The exchange goes on for at least ten minutes on the outer stretch of the main field as Dan does not lose focus of the two young men. Intrigued to say the least, he wants to know exactly who this boy is and why he has never seen him before.

Dan decides to break away from the practice and make a formal introduction to the pair. He gives a gesture with his index finger up to Rick to communicate "be back in one sec." Rick nods. The coach heads over to the boys slowly, adjusting his shirt and glasses to ensure his first impression is impactful. As he approaches, the weaker of the two whispers to the other, "Whoa dude, that's Coach Dan. He's coming over here, I think." The young men straighten up and stand a little taller as the coach appears within conversation distance. Dan politely says, "Nice arm kid. Where'd you learn to throw like that?" Dan obviously and intentionally speaking to the stronger of the two. The boy sheepishly looks down and replies, "I don't know. It's just natural, I guess." Dan replies firmly, hoping the boy would mirror his confidence, "Well, your natural ability is mighty impressive. My name is Dan Butler, but you can call me Coach Dan, head coach of the championship Tigers ten years running. And you are?" The stronger replies, "Yes sir, my name is Jarvis." The weaker boy chimes in from behind, "And I'm Corey sir; nice to meet you." "Pleasure to meet you boys." The coach is being polite, even acknowledging Corey's presence but has no interest in him at all. "Are you a student here, Jarvis?" Dan inquires. Jarvis responds, "Transferring over next year sir; I'm just finishing out my year at Ridgeland. Me and my mom just moved here last week." Corey chimes in, "I already live here sir, almost a year now. Me and Jarvis grew up on the same block back in Ridgeland; he's my best friend." The coach ignores Corey but takes in all the information as useful, something Dan does with everyone he meets. The coach maintains his focus on the stronger boy. "Jarvis." The "R" is silent when Dan says his name, due to his thick southern accent. "I would love to have you try out with our team. I think you have a bright future in football. Did I mention we won the state championship last year?" He does not want to scare Jarvis off, so Dan intentionally positions himself so that Jarvis cannot see the mayhem happening behind him. Kids are vomiting from exhaustion, begging to go home, and passing out on the field. Jarvis replies with skepticism in his tone, "Yes sir, I know. Everyone knows about the Tigers, but I would have to talk to my mom first. I don't think she is going to let me do it this time. I asked before, and she flat out said no." Corey chimes in, "We can both try out. I'll talk to her for you." The coach takes mental note of this dynamic and soon realizes he will need to take them both if he even has a shot of getting the one. He now understands he will have to play nice with Corey to get to Jarvis. "Well, you boys run along now. I will be seeing you around campus. Don't be strangers. I'm going to be looking for you both to be a part of the team this upcoming season." The boys yell "yes sir!" as they run off in delight, excited that one of the most popular men in town asked them to tryout with the championship Tiger football program. Dan waves and starts back over to Rick and the tryout drills. Dan knows he has his work cut out trying to get Jarvis on the team, but he must capitalize on this unexpected bounty that has been presented in his time of need.

CHAPTER 4

"THE TYRANT"

Dan has been thinking about Jarvis ever since he met him. The feeling he has is borderline obsessive. Dan knows that Jarvis can be molded into a star player under his guidance, but he must devise a plan to get him into his summer training camp. There isn't much time, so things need to move rather quickly. But there are important affairs Dan must attend to first so he can focus on Jarvis. The first of which is this board meeting that he has been trying to avoid. Today is Friday, and students at Heritage Park High are released at noon so administrators can attend the board meeting at 1:00 p.m. Dan always dreads these sessions, as it usually places him in contention with everyone in the room because of the massive budget that Dan requires for his football program. The attendees try to tread lightly around Dan knowing his explosive personality, but they need funds badly for other departments; and Dan is unwilling to come off a single dime for his football program. Dan is hoping he will not need to resort to cheap shots and insults in the meeting, but things often go left when budgetary discussions begin.

The group of sixty-eight personnel assemble in a large meeting room behind the main auditorium. This area of the school is part of a beautiful new addition of an otherwise old and outdated structure, just completed nine months ago. The teachers have quickly made this their favorite place to hang out because the bathrooms off the side are new and clean, and the vending machines in this area have the best snacks. Overall, considered a comfortable place to gather. All the teachers have filed in and get seated, waiting for the particulars to begin. Dan always sits in the rear to avoid confrontation. Marcy, who is seated up front, turns to scan the room. She spots Dan amid the crowd, quickly turns back front facing with a sudden timid look on her face. Dan gives a brief grin, still reeling from the interaction he and Marcy had earlier in the week. The vice principal initiates the meeting with an introduction of its organizers. Dan is immediately uninterested and begins to zone out to the point of falling asleep. They start out by going over policy changes and implementing a culture of inclusion with the influx of new Black students for the upcoming year. With about 21% of the student body being black now, this is definitely worth addressing. No one openly voiced any discontent with this subject matter, but you could clearly feel the agitation in the room. There are only two Black teachers in the entire school, and they are usually together when not in their respective classrooms.

Blah, blah, blah is Dan's take on the assembly as he is constantly checking his watch. He has one more very important piece of business he needs to take care of once this snooze-fest is complete. Finally, the last item on the docket, the budget distributions for the upcoming school year. Dan knows he will undoubtedly be the center of this conversation, so he makes a concerted effort to perk up and appear interested. But this time, Dan is in shock when all in attendance agree to the proposed distribution. There will be an increase of $25,000 allotted for Dan's department, money he earned by leading his team to state championships and winning. Dan had forgotten all about the allocation and immediately began to think of self-indulgent ways to spend it. "Meeting adjourned," shouted the assistant principal as everyone began to stand up and file out of the large room. A few of Dan's colleagues made it a point to congratulate him on the increased funds his football program will collect. They pat him on the back and present huge smiles as he hastily tries to maneuver through the crowd. "Thank you, thank you. I appreciate it," Dan responds to each of them without breaking his stride. He finally makes it to the parking lot and inside his car. He just sits for a few minutes, not moving, barely breathing, just bracing for the next task at hand. One he has been putting off for almost three years but must face what may even be for the last time in his life. Dan takes a deep breath, starts his car, puts it in gear, and heads to the nursing home to visit retired US Army Major, David Butler, his father.

Visiting hours at the facility that houses Dan's father are over at 6:00 p.m., so he makes it a point to arrive closer to this time so he will not have long to stay. Dan pulls into the parking lot around 4:30, as he figures this will give him some time to meet with staff, doctors, and administrators to make sure his father's paperwork and overall care needs are being met. The remaining time will be spent with his father, "the Tyrant!" David Butler has been known by the name "the Tyrant" most of his adult life, for good and bad reasons, mostly bad. Dan has this plan clearly mapped out in his head as he approaches the entrance of St. Lucy's Veteran Hospital and Retirement Home. The facility isn't that nice or clean, but it's good enough, especially for "the Tyrant." The walls are a pale green, half tile, half plaster down the long dimly lit hallway Dan must walk to get to the receptionist desk that houses retired veteran residents. The more Dan walks, the more nervous he becomes about seeing his father, who he has not visited in years now. Dan finally approaches a corridor with a sign above labeled "Convalescent Residents." He steps through the large open double doors to a seating area with magazines and coloring books sprawled over a large coffee table. To the right is a clipboard and pen to sign in. A receptionist sits at a desk behind a large, thick glass barrier that she must push a button to speak through. She greets Dan through the glass "Hello sir, are you here visiting someone today?" Dan replies, "Yes ma'am, my father." She cheerfully replies, "Okay sir, just fill out the information on the clipboard in front of you: your name, today's date, person you are visiting, and the check in time, which is approximately 5:34 p.m. I will also need to see a photo ID when you are done." Dan nods as he writes in the information requested by the lady behind the glass. Dan places his ID on top of the clipboard as she grabs it through a small hole at the bottom of the glass. She looks at the ID then looks at the clipboard, and her facial expression can't hide her shock. Dan is not fazed by her reaction as he waits for the return of his ID. She slips the card back under the glass and says, "We will let you back in just a bit sir. Please have a seat." She hops up from the chair and out of the tiny room, obviously to alert the entire staff that someone, anyone, his only son, is here to see "the Tyrant."

The receptionist returns to the tiny room about ten minutes later, out of breath. She speaks to Dan through the glass "Okay, Mr. Butler, you're all set for your visit; your father is in room 119B, straight through these doors on your left. I will buzz you in." Dan nods at the receptionist as he stands and exits the empty waiting area. He enters the doors, and there are nurses and staff huddled around whispering. Dan ignores their behavior, as he is used to this type of reaction with regards to anything that involves his father. One thing Dan cannot ignore is the sinking feeling in his stomach. This is due in part to Dan's eternal fear of his father and the putrid smell emanating from every inch of the hallway. As he progresses to his father's room, which is in view, he passes many amputees, mostly old, some younger. The sights in this area are almost unbelievable. To glance into a room is to see an elderly man, balled up in a bed with soiled covers and a TV with all static and no picture. The nurses are overworked and underpaid, so the residents suffer, after risking their lives for our freedoms. These are mostly veterans from World War II, but some of the younger residents are from the more recent Vietnam War. The images are staggering to Dan, but he must keep his composure for what is yet to come. Dan slowly approaches room 119B, labeled as such because the room is supposed to house two residents, but due to the war hero status "the Tyrant" carries, he is approved to occupy the room alone. Dan sets his sights on his father, who's fighting two nurses who appear to be attempting a bath. "Get your hands off me you cunt bitch," yelled "the Tyrant" in a dull, raspy voice. Though he is not very old, years of constant chain-smoking, extreme alcohol abuse, and hard living have left David Butler a shell of the man he used to be. He used to stand about six feet tall, slim but slightly muscular, with a rigid military posture. Now, he is feeble in mind and body. Small, in comparison to what Dan remembers growing up or even his last visit some years back. Major Butler continues to put on a scene and does not realize that his son is standing in the doorway. The nurses see him but make it a point to continue with their duties while he is watching. If he were not there, they would have surely left him stewing in his own urine for days.

The room is small and cramped to the brim with all Major Butler's prized possessions, or what little is left. Most of the items he has either lost, gambled away, given away, or was stolen. Tons of Nazi memorabilia that Dan vividly remembers growing up in a house with his father. Most of what is left are medals of honor, very large Nazi swords and helmets, his tattered battle uniform, some old clothes, and pictures of him with many beautiful women at various times of his life. Dan has a few items at his house, all that he cared to take once his father was forced into the nursing home after burning up the kitchen. Major Butler suffers from Alzheimer's that started early when he was around fifty-nine, and it has progressively gotten worse as time went on. Dan can hardly ever remember a time when his father wasn't drinking, smoking, or beating him while growing up. He developed a true fear of his father's erratic behavior from the time he was about five years old to as long as he can remember. Dan did have a mother at some point, but the general consensus is that she simply disappeared when Dan was about four years old. His father used to say she just up and left, probably went back to her home country of Greece. But when "the Tyrant" was really drunk, he would jokingly say that she may be buried in the backyard. Dan always believed that his father probably got rid of her as some would recall how bad "the Tyrant" used to beat her and humiliate her. He would taunt her poor speech and broken English. By all accounts, she was a natural beauty, and she truly loved Dan. But David would torture her to no end. She tried her best to shield Dan from the torment, but it would make "the Tyrant" even worse. David brought her home with him from the war; she was a nurse, and he was being treated for several gunshot wounds at the time. Many say the war triggered something evil in him as he was a fine, upstanding, young man prior to his time in

World War II. He gained the name, "the Tyrant," during the battle because of his extreme bravery. He is said to have saved countless lives single-handedly during numerous raids and combat exchanges. He was one of the most decorated soldiers of his platoon, and he would never shut up about it. He would drink too much and go on and on about battle stories, killing hundreds of German soldiers (the number would fluctuate depending on how drunk he was), raping women, and sheep. Yes, sheep! His father had no filter and would readily shout about having intimate relations with farm animals, young girls, and women while stationed in Europe. It didn't matter if Major David was in a room full of political dignitaries, or even if their wives were present. He was so crass, tacky, and blunt, hence the name, "the Tyrant," which stuck with him long after the war.

Dan just sat in the doorway and watched the chaos that was ensuing between his father and the poor nurses. His father was drooling, cursing, and kicking as they had barely gotten past getting his soiled clothes off, much less bathing. The room had an unbelievable stench, but Dan was used to this smell as his dad had been soiling himself almost Dan's whole life. Dan remembers countless beatings growing up at the hands of his alcoholic father. Dan himself entered college at just sixteen years old just to get away from him. Although his father never sexually abused him, Dan remembers his father taking advantage of anyone weaker than him. Dan's mind starts to wander as his father continues to brutalize the nurses. Dan recalls a time when he was about thirteen, the moment he realized just how much of a tyrant his father truly was. One summer day, at the house on Grafton Avenue, the house he and his father lived in, Dan arrived home unexpectedly from a summer job working on a neighbor's farm. Dan was a field hand at the Blandy Ranch about a mile from where he and his father lived. Dan walked in looking for his father so he could avoid him while getting some money he had hidden. Dan wanted to go to the movies straight after work and knew he would be cutting it close if he went home after work, so he sacrificed his lunch break.

When Dan was about to leave, he heard a strange noise off to the side of the house. Dan tiptoed to a window near where he heard the noise. Certain it was his dad; he took extra precautions not to be seen. He slowly pulled back the curtain and made sure almost none of himself was visible to the outside of the window. What he saw would haunt his mind for years to come. The image of what was transpiring outside that day devastated and altered Dan's entire life after that point. There was a young Black neighborhood kid named Joseph who used to come and do yard work for David every two weeks. He was maybe two or three years older than Dan himself at the time, no more than seventeen years old. He was friendly and cordial to Dan when he saw him. But today, he had a look of terror and distress on his face as Major Dan had Joseph on his knees, forcing the young man to perform oral sex on him. Shocked to death, Dan could barely get his thoughts together. He wanted to cry, shout, and vomit all at the same time. He knew his dad had done some horrific things in his time but nothing like this. Dan, for some reason, could not stop looking at what was happening. Though, he felt like he wanted to, he just continued to watch. At one point, it seemed as if Joseph saw Dan in the window, as he was facing the direction of the window, and his father's back was to his view. A tear rolled down Joseph's eye as Major Dan climaxed, tightly gripping the back of his neck so that he could not move until he was done.

He then helped Joseph up and paid him for the yard work as if nothing happened.

Dan rushed out of the front door and ran as fast as he could in the opposite direction of where his father and Joseph were so they would not see him. Once completely out of sight of the house, he slowly walked back to work. For the rest of the day, and the rest of his life for that matter, he wondered how Joseph could allow this to happen. What makes a human being so weak that they just allow someone like his dad to take advantage of them? Joseph wasn't weak or small by any means. He could've overpowered "the Tyrant" if he wanted to, but he didn't. He simply allowed Maj0r Butler to terrorize him. Dan's father terrorized everyone in the community. He would say demeaning and vulgar things about a woman right in front of her husband. He would grope and grind on upstanding women in public. Just about every despicable act you could think of, but this was a new low, even for "the Tyrant." How come no one ever talked about the way he was? Was his father queer? Being homosexual was not something that was tolerated during this time. You just didn't do things like that. Was Joseph queer too? Even though Dan never saw his father do anything like that again, the image stuck in his mind forever. The desperation on poor Joseph's face. Why didn't he beat up "the Tyrant?" Why didn't Joseph bite his penis off and throw it at him? Why did he continue to come over and cut the grass for years after that? And why did Joseph never look Dan or his father in the eyes ever again after that point? Over time, Dan began to realize the psychological mindset of broken people who could be manipulated due to their status in society. Major Butler often spoke of how Black people should have taken over the United States years ago. "If the niggers had a strong mind, they could've made us slaves by now, but the darkies too damn weak for their own good." These words, along with what he saw that day stained his mind and eventually caused him to think and feel just as his father did. Dan was not as brazen about his actions or nearly as boorish or brute. But he was definitely his father's child.

All the time Dan spent at the nursing home, just for his father to tire out after fighting the nurses for forty-five minutes and suddenly fall asleep. The staff assured Dan that his father would not recognize him anyway. His condition had worsened a great deal since Dan last saw him. Dan knew this would probably be the last time that he saw his father alive as the doctor on staff informed him that his father may not make it through the year at the rate he is deteriorating. Dan didn't blink an eye as he processed this information. All of Dan's life, his father treated him poorly. All of Dan's formative years were filled with extreme physical and emotional abuse. Once Dan was too big to beat on, his father constantly berated him with verbal taunts. Some of the most crude, profane, and obscene language a person could use toward someone, much less their own child. Even calling his son a "faggot" for choosing education over the military and not defending America in the Vietnam War. "The tyrant" would often question if Dan were even his son, though, they bore many similar features. It was a drunken old man's only weapon, the mighty tongue. Dan finally washed his hands of his father during a visit to the nursing home, and "the Tyrant" scolded and spit on him in front of his wife and kids. That was the end in Dan's mind, but this was the indefinite end. Dan is very proud of his career and his family, but he is not proud of how his father's indiscretions shaped his life and his mentality. Major David Butler, "the Tyrant," will have to live out his final days at the mercy of strangers, as Dan will never return to see his father again.

Major David, "the tyrant," Butler died two weeks later, Dan and his family did not attend his services.

CHAPTER 5

"INVESTIGATING THE PROSPECT"

Dan is more than ready to get back to work and feeling invigorated, after some much needed time off. Since all the chaos surrounding his father's death had finally waned, Dan now has time and opportunity to direct his full focus on Jarvis. Dan used his bereavement leave and a bit of personal time he had accumulated, not to grieve the loss of his dad, but to hatch out a well-designed plan to get closer to Jarvis without coming off like the creep he actually is. Dan had written out pages of detailed plans for chance and prepared meetings with Jarvis. Stakeouts, inconspicuous surveillance, and intense observations are all meticulously crafted in this handwritten manifesto that Dan guarded with his life. He had a small, square, leather briefcase that he usually starts carrying around this time of the year. It has a lockable code wheel that only Dan knows. Almost everyone assumes it is for top secret plays that the coach had written up and did not want leaked. That case carries far more sinister information. Dan spends most of his time away from work in his home office, under the guise that he is extremely stressed and profoundly mourning the loss of his father. Behind the closed, locked door, his father never crossed his mind. His thoughts were exceedingly centered on Jarvis, every waking moment in fact. He is able to hide his alternate life from his family due to the fact Dan has always been distant and secretive. It came off as an introspective passion for his job. No one, including his family, ever questioned his often-reclusive personality. His wife and kids started to expect this behavior from him during the summer months and did their best to just give him as much space as possible. With their own busy lives in place, and the death of "the Tyrant," Dan's increasingly strange habits have all but gone unnoticed in the Butler household.

It is the end of May, and with only a couple of weeks left in the school year, Dan decides it is time to put his plan in motion. Jarvis does not yet attend Heritage Park High, so Dan has to rely on chance encounters after school. Jarvis also does not show up every single day, so Coach Dan knows he has to make the most of every interaction with him. This is all a part of Dan's intense and methodical grooming process which he has perfected at this point. Having practiced many times over through trial and error over the years, Dan has an almost flawless system worked out with his targets. Grooming is not something that Dan takes lightly. He puts most of his time and effort into learning any and every detail about his game (he viewed his grooming process as a sport). Once he has gathered all the personal ammunition, he needs regarding one's entire life, he is armed and ready to start intense social interaction with his prey. There's usually little resistance once the reciprocal intercommunication has started given Dan's status in the community and ability to present himself as non-threatening. Once at his home, full advantage is taken, and there is almost nothing that can be done to avoid what is inevitable. Dan does not attack these situations with the brute force of his father; he is far more calculated. These boys will likely hold these secrets for life, because Dan has threatened to tell lies to the community about their actions and keep them from a promising future in collegiate and possibly professional sports. Opportunities these young Black men needed so badly during this time. Dan is far more menacing than any threat these young men faced in their lives at this time. His insatiable appetite for these boys could undoubtedly pose a threat to Dan's comfortable life as he knows it. But a young, athletic, handsome, and intelligent Jarvis is well within Dan's sights and worth the consequences.

Dan pretty much goes through the motions on his first day back at work. Of course, there is the constant barrage of "so sorry for your loss" and "my deepest condolences to you, Dan" and the most awkward of all, "your father was a good man." *Fucking liars,* thought Dan, knowing well enough no one in Heritage Park liked his dad. He just nodded and said thank you each time. Everyone assumed Dan was saddened over the loss of his father, which allowed him some much-needed peace without being disturbed. He sat in his office counting down to the time when he would hopefully meet with Jarvis and methodically start executing his plan. Dan begins packing up his already tidy desk area and grabs his suitcase to start his early departure toward the practice field. Just as he is about to exit his office, he is suddenly greeted by Rick, which extremely startles Dan. Rick apologizes profusely for alarming Dan but seems genuinely excited that he is back. Rick verbalizes his condolences about his father's passing and without taking a breath, launches full force into all the juicy gossip that Dan has missed during his time away. Normally, Dan would be highly interested in such hearsay, but today, he is distracted. The two walk to the practice field, Rick babbling a mile a minute. Dan just nods occasionally, barely acknowledging his presence. Then finally, at the end of all that meaningless chatter, Rick says something that catches Dan's attention. "Oh, and that kid that's always hanging around practice, Javis, Jay or whatever his name is, he and his little goofy friend are committed to summer practice. I got him to join while you were out." Dan could hardly hide his excitement as a partial smile appeared on his face, which was the extent of emotion you would get out of him. Part of his plan was already done for him thanks to Rick. Dan now knows he will have significant time to spend getting to know Jarvis on a personal level.

School has now let out for the day, and Dan watches as Rick leads the practice drills. Dan anxiously awaits the arrival of Jarvis, who is late. Rick has already informed Dan of Jarvis' exception for tardiness, as he has to travel from the inner-city school district until he is enrolled at Heritage Park. Around 4:30 p.m., Dan spots what appears to be Jarvis off in the distance, walking across the front lawn of the school entrance. He has on a pair of athletic shorts, a light blue printed t-shirt, white socks with stripes at the top, pulled up to his calf, and an old pair of Jordan sneakers. He appears to have a newer pair sticking out of his bag. His clothes appear pressed and neatly arranged on his slim, athletic body. Dan makes mental notes of these things. Unlike most of the Black kids in and around Heritage Park, Jarvis obviously has parents that care about his appearance and have money to buy him nice things. This will pose a minor hurdle, as kids who have caring parents are more likely to resist advances from adults like Dan. One of the main reasons Dan has never targeted white boys in the area. But he is so invested at this point, he accepts it as a welcomed challenge. As the figure gets closer to the practice field, Dan establishes that is in fact Jarvis, and he is even more beautiful than he remembers. The summer sun has caused his lighter skin to turn a beautiful reddish-brown tint, which is glistening from a light sweat. The neat close fade he had last time Dan saw him had grown out a bit into beautiful, thick black curls. He is just a bit shorter than most kids his age, standing only about five feet, seven inches tall, but all legs. His posture is perfect. His body is also naturally muscular but very lean. In Dan's mind, he is a vision of perfection, and he is more impressed with Jarvis than before.

Dan's mirrored Aviator shades hide the excitement in his eyes as Jarvis makes his way towards Dan and the other players. Jarvis removes his walk-man headphones and extends his hand to Coach Dan to gesture a handshake. Dan takes note of this as well. Jarvis is well mannered and comfortable interacting with adults. This is going to be harder than Dan initially thought. Dan wants to hug Jarvis but simply grabbed his hand in a very firm handshake which is returned to Dan with an equally firm grip. There is eye contact as Jarvis speaks to Dan, "Nice to see again Coach. I heard about your father, and I am so very sorry for your loss. My deepest condolences to you and your family." Dan was speechless at how articulate and thoughtful Jarvis was. This is also unique to boys his age as Dan senses a high level of maturity and confidence. Dan is starting to realize Jarvis is definitely not like most boys his age. "Thank you, Jarvis. That means a lot; it's really good to see you again as well!" Dan is floored by the exchange he just had with Jarvis. Dan motions for him to hit the field with the rest of the players as Jarvis is placing his personal items on a nearby bench. The coach is elated at the thought of breaking down every admirable trait Jarvis has and making him a personal slave in every imaginable way. Dan wants athletic, mental, and physical control of Jarvis but understands he has his work cut out for him. He realizes that Jarvis' parental figures have a high level of control, and he must form a wedge in that bond for this to work. *It's going to be a long but fun summer*, thinks Dan.

Dan has slowed down on his original plan, which was swift and aggressive. He must now execute a more psychological approach, which requires more research on Jarvis' family life. Most of the young boys from Dan's past indiscretions came from more sorted home lives and exhibited a lack of confidence that relaxed them to Dan's control. Dan has resigned himself to spending evenings finding out every detail about Jarvis' personal situation. This includes stalking every minute of Jarvis' day. In just four short days, Dan already deeply understands Jarvis' scheduled routine. Dan has allowed Rick to take over as "Practice Coordinator," a made-up title so that Rick can feel important and do Dan's job for no increase in pay. With tons of free time on his hands, Dan started following Jarvis home immediately that week after practice. This is how Dan found out which of the many new apartment complexes he lives in. Dan is back out early the next day to watch as Jarvis leaves the apartment for school. It looks as if Jarvis exits his home early to catch the 7:35 a.m. bus into the city. The bus doesn't have many stops before it arrives five blocks from Ridgeland Central Senior High School, where Jarvis is a rising 11th grader. Jarvis usually hops off the bus around 8:10 a.m., just enough time to quickly walk the three blocks and be on time for homeroom at 8:30 a.m. Dan doesn't dare be seen by Jarvis or any of the area locals, as he is easily recognizable all over the city. Dan kills time running errands and pretending to be busy at work until it's time for Jarvis to exit classes at 3:30 p.m. where he waits for the 3:50 bus back to Heritage Park.

The walk from the Heritage Park bus stop to the high school is longer than Dan remembered from the previous night. Jarvis is much more disciplined and mature than Dan originally thought. For almost a split second, Dan felt bad for the intentions he had for Jarvis and the long-term effects it may have on his life. But those feelings all but faded every time he set eyes on the young man. He is a sight to behold, and the coach isn't the only one to notice. The coach quietly observes as Jarvis seems to have an abundance of female admirers at both schools. Both Black and white girls at Heritage Park gathered at the practices to watch him play. Jarvis mostly wore shorts that hit just about mid-thigh in length, always tight, which Dan really liked. Along with a t-shirt that had cut off sleeves and bottom to show off his muscular arms and stomach, popular fashion in the eighties. Dan has obtained so much information about Jarvis from Monday to Thursday and has decided he will take things a step further on Friday by initiating a one-on-one conversation with him. This will be the last step before extending the football camp invite. Dan will just need the last piece of the puzzle, to find out more about Jarvis' father.

With all this newfound information, Dan is certain the rest of his plan will be smooth sailing. Dan even knows that Jarvis' mom is an E.R. nurse at the nearby St. Peter Hospital, a position not commonly held by Black people during this time. Especially not in the majority white, Heritage Park. This tells Dan that they aren't struggling like most of the Black people who have transitioned to the area. He also knows Jarvis' mom's name and her shift hours at the hospital. Her name is Naomi Robinson (everyone calls her Nae), a short, slim brown woman with long, beautiful hair. She appears to be very young to have a son Jarvis' age. Early thirties at the oldest but looks much younger than that. She seems dedicated to her role at the hospital and well respected by her peers. Dan has witnessed Nae and other staff outside the hospital on smoke breaks laughing and joking. She works an overnight shift, from 8:00 p.m. until around 4:00 a.m., and doesn't seem to take many days off. Jarvis is alone during much of this time but does not appear to take advantage of his relaxed situation, as Dan has never seen him exit the property after dusk. This also speaks to his high level of maturity for his young age. Everything that Dan has learned in this very short amount of time has given great insight into how to approach Jarvis about the upcoming "summer camp" at Dan's house. There is still that one small piece to the puzzle that Dan must be certain of before moving completely forward. Where is Jarvis' father, and what role does he play in Jarvis' life? Dan knows that the absence of Jarvis' father will make things a lot easier in the long run, but he hasn't seen any sign of him. He had to have been present at some point as Dan knows that Jarvis is a Jr and does not have the same last name as his mother. Dan will need to dig a bit deeper for information on Jarvis Sr.

Jarvis Sr. is quite the mystery, but Dan is running out of time as the end of the school year is only one week away. It is Friday evening, and Dan decides it's finally time to have that one-on-one conversation he had been looking forward to. Practice is almost over, and Dan had worked the living SHIT out of his practice squads! Rick blows the whistle for practice to be over, and the exhausted bunch drag themselves over to the bleachers for a quick rest before heading home. A few kids already had rides waiting, and the older kids either had their own cars or rode with a teammate with their own car. Basically, the kids are vacating the premises pretty fast. Rick's clearing off the practice field, so Dan walks over to the bleachers where Jarvis and Corey are sitting. "Nice practice guys," said Dan, trying to include Corey, even though he loathed him for being weak and slow. They both responded in unison, "Thank you sir," Corey said much louder than Jarvis. Dan paused as if to choose his words very carefully. "Jarvis," he started in his southern dialect, "once you're done here, I'd like to have quick chat with you about something; it'll only take a minute." Dan knows that he plans to hold Jarvis for a good amount of time, but he wants Corey to leave so he could pry more information out of Jarvis and plant the seed for staying at his home for the summer. Dan basically tells Corey to "beat it" as he places his hand on Jarvis' shoulder, walking him towards the front of the school where the buses load and parents pull in to pick up their kids. Corey looks puzzled as he just sits watching the coach and Jarvis get further and further away. There are almost no students left on site as the sunlight starts to dim and shade. It's about 6:00 p.m., and Dan knows he doesn't have long to speak so he makes it count.

Jarvis sits on the edge of a sizeable cement slab, just outside of the massive double doors where the students make their way to the buses. Dan leans over the metal rails, still standing, but bent over enough so that he and Jarvis can talk. "Javis, how is school going for you? Are you passing your classes at Ridgeland?" "Yes sir," Jarvis responds quickly. "A-B honor roll sir. My mama wouldn't have it any other way." "That's a good boy. Listen to your mama; I'm sure she's a smart lady." "Yes sir, she definitely is that!" Jarvis replies with great pride and enthusiasm when it comes to conversation about his mom. Dan is still leaning over, looking down at Jarvis while Jarvis is looking down as well, swinging his feet at least five feet above the ground. Dan, realizing the conversation is growing stale decides to come right out and ask Jarvis about his dad. "Jarvis, do you ever talk to your dad at all?" Jarvis stops swinging his feet, looks up at Dan and says, "Sure I do! He's on the way to pick me up now. I stay at his house on the weekends." Dan is shocked! Here he was assuming Jarvis didn't have a father present in his life. He should've known better as exceptional of a young man he is. "Oh, I didn't mean anything by asking you that; it's just that I never see him. I wasn't sure. I'm sorry if I offended you," said Dan, realizing his questioning may have come off as stereotypical. Jarvis, who never broke eye contact since looking up at Dan, cracks a small smile and says, "It's all good Coach!" Dan smiles back and asks Jarvis when his father will be arriving; he wants to meet him. Jarvis replies in disgust, "He gets off work around 6, but with traffic, he probably won't get here until 6:30 or so." Dan looks at his watch, and it's 6:17 p.m., just enough time to get some more questions in. "What type of work does your dad do?" asks Dan. Jarvis replies, "I'm not completely sure, but I know he works for a big paper plant on the other side of the city. He ain't no scrub either; he's a big-time supervisor or something." "Ahhh, the Bristol Papermill in Guston. You're right; that is a big deal!" "Yeah, that's it!" Jarvis replies excitedly. "Do you like staying with him on the weekends? Do you all do fun stuff?" Dan is trying to gauge the level of involvement his dad has in Jarvis' life. "Yeah, it's okay. My dad is a real cool guy, a ladies' man too; he always has a bunch of women hanging around, but we still find time to hang out," says Jarvis. Dan, without hesitation, then asks, "How are you with the ladies Jarvis? You got a girlfriend?" "Nah, I mean, there are girls that I like, but they are all older and don't take me seriously," replies Jarvis to Dan's increasingly invasive questioning. "So have you ever had a girlfriend?" Dan really pries at this point. "I mean, kind of, depends how you look at it," Jarvis says with smirk on his face but continues to look down at his dangling feet. "I'm not sure what you mean.

Explain," says Dan. "Well," Jarvis let's out a big sigh as if he's reluctant to tell the coach what he is about to say. "This is embarrassing but you asked," says Jarvis. "There's this girl in school; she's sort of cute, but I don't really like her as a girlfriend completely. Her name is Janice," explains Jarvis. "Lord, she got some big titties; excuse my language Coach." "You're fine, finish your story," the coach chuckles a bit listening to the way Jarvis describes Janice. "Well, for the better part of the year now, we been meeting up in the alley two blocks from school behind some abandoned buildings. There is never anyone around," Jarvis continues. "So maybe twice a week, she lets me feel her titties while she," Jarvis pauses.

Dan is intrigued at the direction this exchange is going, "Uh hmm, while she what Jarvis?" "Plays with it, jerks it. You know what I mean Coach," says Jarvis sheepishly. "Oh yeah, I know exactly what you mean. Do you finish when she does that? Get my drift," asks Dan who is becoming aroused by the dialogue. "Yeah, pretty much every time. I can't help it when I'm feeling on those titties; they are so soft," replies Jarvis in an embarrassed, yet amused tone. Thank goodness Jarvis is looking downward at his feet because Dan has become noticeably excited. Dan has allowed his mind and body to lose control for a moment, but he suddenly snaps out of it realizing that Jarvis' dad would be arriving at any moment. He discreetly adjusts himself and switches the subject quickly before things get out of hand. "So, the reason why I wanted to speak with you is so I could let you know about my summer training camp that I host at my house every year," says Dan. "I choose one player from the practice squad and allow them to stay at my house and train for six weeks, free of charge." "There will be practice sessions, weight training, mentorship, and three meals per day, cooked by my lovely wife. We take care of your laundry and any expenses that occur while under my roof," boasts Dan. "This year, Jarvis, I choose you! How does that sound?" Jarvis' face lights up for about two seconds; he is grinning ear to ear, but in the blink of an eye, his head hangs and a dejected frown replaces what used to be a smile. "I know my mom coach; she definitely is not going to let me do this." There's despair in Jarvis' voice. "Why not?" asks the coach. "Well for one, I go to North Carolina every summer and help out on my great grandparents farm; it's boring, and I hate all that work," squawks Jarvis. "And secondly, she doesn't want me to play football, so I know she ain't going to agree to me staying at some white people's house she never met just so I can play football." Dan sarcastically laughs at the part of Jarvis' rant concerning his race, as if to imply the irony that he be deemed the feared one in this scenario. Though, he actually is. "Well, I can talk to her on your behalf if you like; it really is a good opportunity, and there is a 90% college acceptance rate among the boys who have stayed over the past 10 years. You would really be passing up a major opportunity," explains Dan. Jarvis replies, "I know. Just let me run it past my dad so he can talk to my mom, butter her up. She won't admit it, but she still has a thing for him." Dan replies, "Whatever you want, just try, and let me know by next week. If you don't come, I have to prepare for someone else to take that spot," Dan says, trying to make Jarvis feel guilty. "Okay Coach." "I will let my–" before Jarvis can get the rest of his sentence out, his dad speeds into the bus ramp headed to where Dan and Jarvis are posted.

Blasting loud rap music, he abruptly stops his late model sports coupe directly in front of Dan and Jarvis. His T-tops are open as the evening is warm, even for this time of year. He gestures out of the top of the car for Jarvis to come so they can leave. Jarvis hops down off the steep ramp and starts over to his dad's car. Dan follows but takes the steps instead. They both end up at Jarvis Sr.'s beautiful black car at the same time; it's even more stunning up close. Jarvis' father is just an older version of Jarvis; they look identical. Beautiful white teeth: he appears very tall and extremely handsome. Dan can see why Jarvis labeled his father a "ladies' man." Jarvis Sr. turns his music down as the coach reaches his hand out for a formal greeting. "Hey, I'm Coach Dan. I run the football program here at Heritage Park High School. Jarvis has told me so many good things about you. Pleasure to finally meet you," says Dan in his deceptively pleasant voice. "Likewise!" says Jarvis Sr. "Call me Jay; everybody calls me Jay." "Okay Jay. I just wanted to tell you that you have raised a fine young man here." "I can't take all the credit; his mama does a really good job keeping him in line. Makes my job really easy," laughs Jay. "Well, I won't hold you two. I'm sure you both have fun things planned, but I did want to run by you briefly what Jarvis and I were just talking about," says Dan to a captivated Jay. "Well, I host a football training camp at my house for six weeks to help one well-deserving player get prepared for the upcoming season. That player will stay at my house with my family and me all while training intensively, three meals a day, laundry, and a bit of life training as well, no expense to the parents. This year, I have chosen Jarvis because he shows the most potential out of all the other kids on the practice squad right now. I mean, that's just a brief overview. I can provide a detailed list of activities and references from past players if you like; it's a really good opportunity. I'd hate for Jarvis to miss out," Dan explains to Jay. Jay let's a deep sigh riddled with pessimism, "Well, if it were up to me, it'd be a no brainer. I'd let him stay in a heartbeat. But you DO NOT KNOW HIS MOTHER!" explains

Jay emphatically. "All I can do is try Coach. I'll talk to her this weekend when I drop him back off; she is hellbent on making this boy a sissy," says Jay as he cuts his eye over at Jarvis. "I ain't no damn sissy," Jarvis quietly mumbles under his breath, hoping his dad wouldn't hear him. "What did you say?" Jay firmly barks at Jarvis. "Come on, let's go get something to eat. I'm starving!" Dan doesn't react to the bickering between the two. "Well, it was nice meeting you Jay. Please have that talk with your other half and try to let me know something by next Friday. The camp starts in two weeks, and if Jarvis can't come, I'll have to choose someone else. But understand, he is my first choice!" "Will do Coach." Jay waves through the exposed roof as he and Jarvis back out of the bus ramp with the music blaring. Dan knows he has his work cut out for him, but he has made great strides today with nothing more than a twenty-minute conversation. Dan walks across the empty parking lot to his car as the sun starts to set, feeling accomplished yet at the same time, feeling horny. It was a good day; Dan decides to take the long way home this evening.

CHAPTER 6

"LOW HANGING FRUIT"

The entire weekend had gone by, and Dan hardly slept a wink wondering if Jarvis would be able to stay at his house for the "summer training program." School has already let out, and the practice squads are out running their normal drills with Rick. Dan did not want to seem anxious, but he kept his eyes on a constant lookout for Jarvis walking across the school grounds for practice. Just as Dan is about to take over coaching for a bit, he spots Jarvis moving slowly toward the football field. Dan wants to run over and ask what happened. What did his mother say? But he just casually walks over so that they can speak privately without the rest of the team overhearing. Once Dan gets within a few feet of Jarvis, he nonchalantly says, "Hello Jarvis. I hope you had a fun weekend. You must already know what I'm about to ask." Dan wastes no time getting right to it. Jarvis hangs his head, and if Dan weren't directly in front of him, he wouldn't have heard what he was about to say. "I don't think I'm gonna be able to go Coach," says Jarvis with almost no confidence in his tone. Dan is stunned; he doesn't know what to say! Dan stands silent for about three minutes, the entire time, Jarvis is on the verge of tears. Finally, Dan breaks the silence by asking, "Well, what did she say?" Jarvis tries to regain his composure. "What didn't she say?" he says sarcastically. Dan replies, "What exactly did she give as a reason, Jarvis?" Jarvis reluctantly replies, "Well, basically, she said I don't need to be staying in a house with all of them white folks by myself. Sorry if that offends you Coach." Dan smiled and in a comforting voice so Jarvis wouldn't feel embarrassed. "Is that right? Well, I imagine a hard-working woman like your mama Jarvis never met too many good white people in her life, but I'm good people, regardless of my color, you understand?" says Dan to Jarvis in a soothing voice. "I'm just gonna have to work to change her mind, that's all." "Well good luck," Jarvis bleakly responds. The coach is at a loss and not sure what his next move should be, when suddenly, the answer is right in front of him, literally!

Here comes Corey, Jarvis' best friend, awkwardly barreling directly towards the coach and Jarvis. Corey falls clumsily just a couple of feet in front of the two. The coach is usually annoyed at the sheer presence of Corey, but at this very moment, his timing could not have been more perfect! Dan leans into Jarvis, "How about this? Number one, Corey is invited to the training camp along with you. This way, your mom can feel more comfortable." Dan continues, "And secondly, I would like to personally pay your mom a personal visit so that I can better explain the program to her. How about that?" Jarvis perks up and even gives a little smile at the coach's suggestion. Corey is still rolling around on the ground like a wounded animal but has no visible injuries in sight. Dan firmly yells at Corey, "Get up now! Get over here. I need to talk to you!" Corey slowly drags himself up, dusting the grass and dirt off his clothes and pretending to limp as he approaches Dan and Jarvis. Corey daps Jarvis as they greet one another, the coach paying special attention to their comradery. Corey is not anything like Jarvis, and this is obvious at just first glance.

Corey is tall, thin, and very dark skinned. Corey never appears to be clean, and his body has a stench that is stale and pungent. His clothes are worn to the point of holes, and they do not fit properly. His hair is coarse and matted and never freshly cut like Jarvis. Corey has a chipped yellow tooth in front of all the other jumbled, crooked teeth in his mouth. His lips are always dry and cracked, and when he speaks, sometimes a white froth accumulates in the corners of his mouth. His breath is nauseating most days, which is why Dan can never pay attention to his words. Not with all the chaos surrounding his mouth in general. He doesn't seem to be as articulate or smart as his best friend either. Corey just isn't in the same class as Jarvis, yet it perplexes Dan how close they are. Dan speaks firmly to Corey, "Are you okay?" "Yes sir," replies Corey. "Did Jarvis tell you about my summer training camp?" "Yes sir," replied Corey again. "I know I'm not invited, but I wish I was." "Well, that's all changed. I want you and Jarvis both to come and join me this summer." Before Corey could start into his celebration, the coach interrupts him and says, "But only on one condition." Corey excitedly responds, "Anything coach, you name it!" "That we can convince Jarvis' mom to let him come too. If Jarvis can't come, you can't either." Corey quickly agrees, and the two boys celebrate hysterically. The rest of the team stare in disgust as they are tired and have a good idea what the conversation is about. Dan says to Corey, "Do you think your parents will allow you to participate?" "HELL YEAH!" Corey yells emphatically. "Oops, sorry coach. I meant, of course they will get me out of the house and free food; this is the blessing they been waiting for." As Corey and Jarvis laugh, Dan asks Corey, "Are your parents home now?" Corey responds, "Well, I know at least my mom is, my dad usually goes to the pool hall downtown after work." "Why don't we cut out early today boys, pay her a visit, and we can stop and get some ice cream on the way? How does that sound?" The boys can hardly believe their good fortune as they exuberantly yell "YESSS!" The entire team turns to watch them heading off as the coach gestures to Rick about his departure. Some of kids on the field can be heard mumbling, "Lucky bastards."

The boys are fat and happy as they arrive at Corey's apartment. While they are still inside Dan's car, Dan asks Corey how he should approach the situation, as though he has no prior interaction with his parents. Corey shrugs and jokingly says, "You probably should've brought a bottle; she likes to drink." Corey and Jarvis die laughing in the back seat. The coach barely cracks a smile as he exits the car. "You boys stay here; I'll be right back." The boys' demeanor suddenly become more serious as Jarvis asks Corey, "You think he gonna be alright?" Corey responds, "Should be. My daddy not home; he don't like no men coming to our house when he not there. That nigga will flip out." Corey and Jarvis both hang their heads out of the opposite windows of Dan's car to be nosy as Dan approaches the stoop to Corey's apartment. The coach straightens his shirt and hat as he rings the doorbell and waits for someone to answer. Dan can hear the TV through the door as he stands motionless waiting for at least three minutes. Then finally, the door cracks open, and the smell of cigarettes and beer hits Dan in the face like a left hook.

Once the smoke clears and Dan lets out a few suppressed coughs, a tall, sturdy dark-skinned woman stands peeping out of a small, cracked doorway with a night robe pulled tight to her neck. "Can I help you sir?" She appears to have just woken up as it is barely 6:00 p.m.. "Is this about Corey? Lord, what did that boy do now? I'm gonna beat his ass when I see him!" Dan laughs. "Hello ma'am. My name is Dan Butler, and I am the head football coach at Heritage Park High School. Corey isn't in any trouble; he's actually a fine young man." She rolls her eyes at the coach's portrayal of Corey, as if she knows it's bullshit. "And who do I have the pleasure of speaking with?" asks Dan politely to the woman in the door. "I'm Corey's mom. My name is Jaqueline, but everyone calls me Jackie." Dan holds out his hand to gesture a handshake; Jackie extends just the tips of her fingers out of the door and offers Dan a limp, gripless greeting. Dan grabs her hand and shakes it with an unvarying level of force. "Nice to meet you, Jackie. I won't take up too much of your time this evening. I'm sure you are well aware that Corey is trying out for football this upcoming season." Jackie nods. "Well, I host a training program at my house every summer for one special athletic standout, but this ye —" Before Dan could complete his sentence, Jackie bust out laughing. "You can't be talking about Corey, not my Corey. Corey Tucker?" Jackie asks, amused at just the thought. "That boy don't know his ass from his head. Now tell me what you really want." She is no longer laughing. "Well Miss Jackie, I'm serious. I have chosen Corey and Jarvis to attend this year. I usually only pick one, but this year, I just couldn't decide between the two. So, I am hosting both." Jackie smiles and nods. "You need Corey so Nae will let Jarvis come too." Dan is astonished at how sharp Jackie is! "Well, I mean, umm —" Dan is stuttering and at a loss for words, as Jackie's abrupt tone sharpens as she looks Dan directly in his eyes. "How much is it? I ain't got no extra to spend on his ass this summer." Dan quickly replies, "No ma'am, not a dime out of pocket for you; it's all free: food, clean nice home with my family, over in

45

Beaumont Estates. Heard of it?" Dan strategically name drops his high-class sub-division to relieve some tension in their conversation, and it works! Jackie's whole attitude relaxes as she begins to loosen her robe from around her neck; she cracks the door a little further, and allows one of her long, brown legs to be exposed. She also begins patting and primping her disheveled, bushy hair while showing all her teeth. "Beaumont Estates, huh? I heard of it. Beautiful homes in that area. How long is this summer camp?" Dan replies, "Four weeks ma'am; we wrap up the second week of July; the boys will celebrate the 4th with us." "That's it! You don't want to keep him longer?" Jackie replies with a hearty laugh as she leans into Dan's shoulder. Dan smiles nervously, as Jackie seems a little too comfortable for his taste. "Yes ma'am. The camp starts Monday, a week from today. All Corey needs is a regular change of clothes and toiletries." "No problem, Dan. He will be ready with bells on." Jackie runs her index finger down Dan's chest. Dan steps back a few inches. "Well thank you ma'am; it was nice meeting you. I will have my son pick Corey up Sunday evening if that's all right with you." "That is just fine, and if you need to get in touch with me for any reason, just get the number from Corey. It's best if you call during the day," Jackie says seductively as Dan stumbles backwards while quickly exiting the porch.

Dan walks fast and hastily gets back to the car where the boys are in the back seat laughing uncontrollably! "What's so funny?" Dan aggressively turns to the rear of the car where the boys are. "My mama is a trip Coach Dan. I think she got a crush on you too. You better get on out this parking lot before Milton get home!" "Who is Milton?" asks Dan. Corey responds matter-of-factly, "That's my daddy, and that nigga do not play about my mama! Excuse my language coach, but my daddy is crazy!"

Corey hops out of the coach's car but leans inside the passenger window and says, "Y'all better go before he gets home. I'm serious; he knows how my mama is, and if he knows you was here coach, he'll beat you to death with his bare hands." The coach and Jarvis wave goodbye to Corey. Jarvis yells, "See you at practice tomorrow fag" as they speed off. Corey nods, holding up his middle finger as he heads into the house. Jarvis lives in the same cluster of apartments as Corey but about a tenth of a mile further down. Dan pulls into the empty parking space directly beside Jarvis' mom's car. Dan asks Jarvis, "Can I come talk to her now?" Jarvis replies, "She's probably resting or getting ready for work, and even if she isn't, it's probably not a good time." "Well, when is a good time?" asks Dan. "I don't know honestly. Probably when she's at work, but I don't expect you to see her at two o'clock in the morning," says Jarvis. "You don't worry about it. I have an idea; it'll be fine," Dan reassures Jarvis. "Thanks Coach, you're the best!" Jarvis exits Dan's car and he briefly turns to wave before heading inside the house. Dan takes a deep breath as he reflects on all the excitement of the day. The sun is starting to set on Heritage Park as Coach Dan finally heads home. During the brief ride to his house, Dan thinks about Jarvis and how beautiful, smart, and athletic he is. In that same moment, he wonders how Jarvis can be such good friends with a loser like Corey. He lacks every positive quality that Jarvis effortlessly possesses, yet they are almost inseparable. Dan had decided early on, that though Corey was an easy target, low hanging fruit in other words, he would not dare touch him or even treat him with nearly the same dignity as Jarvis. Corey is simply there because Dan has no other way to get Jarvis to his home without him. Dan loathes Corey's very existence and is honestly disgusted to have him in his home, but what else could he do? Can't dwell on it.

What's done is done, and he must get some rest before attacking his most challenging task yet.

Brrrinngg! a noisy alarm clock sounds and startles Dan out of his deep and satisfying sleep. Groggy and not fully alert, he sits up after falling asleep on a small sofa in his home office. He stops the alarm and checks the time, 1:45 a.m. Dan knows that he does not have a lot of time, as he has planned to meet Nae, Jarvis' mom, at her job to speak about the training camp. After all the excitement that took place earlier in the day, Dan is ready for just about anything. There is a level of fear Dan has about approaching Nae at her place of employment unexpectedly, but with time running low, he feels that he has no other choice. Dan is already dressed when he awakes, so no time is wasted as he quietly slips out of the back door, careful not to alert his wife and kids. He had purposely parked on the street when he arrived home earlier that evening knowing that pulling off at 2:00 a.m. would generate a certain amount of noise that could potentially rouse those in the Butler household. Dan had thought of everything as he pulls off into the cool night air. Dan arrives at the hospital parking lot around 2:05 a.m.. He sits in his car with a clear view of the door he had previously seen Nae come out of for her cigarette break just the week before. Dan felt as though Nae should be walking out at any moment and had timed her break perfectly. However, that was not the case. During his wait, Dan managed to neatly comb his hair while looking in his rear-view mirror.

He must've chewed at least six sticks of gum in his first ten minutes of sitting there; he was always self-conscious about his breath. Dan had been waiting for almost an hour and was starting to wish he had a large cup of coffee, as his eyes are getting extremely heavy. Dan looks at his watch and sees that it is ten minutes after 3 a.m. To make sure Nae is actually at work for her shift that evening, Dan decides to make a quick loop to the employee parking lot to see if her car is there; this is also an effort to wake him up as well. Dan does not even have to drive completely into the employee lot, as her blue 1984 Ford Escort is the first car visible. Dan hastily hurries back to the entrance where he was originally parked now that he has confirmation of her presence. Just as he pulls back into his spot, Nae and two coworkers walk out the door Dan has been watching. Dan suddenly has a sinking feeling in the pit of his stomach, but it's now or never as he exits the driver side of his car. Dan takes a deep breath as he approaches them, all three smoking at this point. Before Dan could even get within clear view of the workers, one of them loudly says, "Coach Dan, what are you doing here?" It is one of the three smokers, a short, youthful, white girl with her blonde hair pulled into a ponytail and pair of blue scrubs on. Dan does not recognize her but smiles as he approaches. "Hello everybody. I'm fine. Good to see you young lady." Everybody seemed friendly and generally happy to see the coach, except Nae, suddenly realizing who he is. The young lady who had called out to Dan launches into an introduction once it registers to her that no one else standing there probably has any idea who he is. "This is Coach Dan, the legend, and the award-winning head football coach at Heritage Park High. I'm Class of 83." A tall, effeminate male is one of the three standing with them. He seemed friendly but unimpressed with the grand introduction and eager to leave the situation. "Nice to meet you," says the young man as he quickly puts his barely smoked cigarette out in the ashtray and heads off into the building. "Going to check on Mr. Gough in 113." The blonde and Nae are left standing with the coach. The blonde breaks the awkward silence. "So, coach, are you here visiting someone?" she speaks confidently, assuming the coach remembers who she is, but he doesn't. "Actually, I'm here on business. I kind of need to speak with Miss Naomi here about her amazing son," Dan responds. Nae looks up, shocked at the coach's explanation of why he was there. The blonde surprisingly responds, "Well Nae, you never told me Jarvis was a football star. Let me get out of your way; good to see you Coach Dan. See you in a few hon."

Now, with only Dan and Nae outside, Dan starts off with an apology. "Miss Naomi, let me first start off by saying how sorry I am for barging in on your job at 3:00 a.m.; this must be very unsettling for you, but I didn't have any other good time to meet you with your work schedule." Naomi's face is that of disgust, speaking volumes in her silence. The coach notices how sweet and pretty she is now that he is up close; he sees so much of Jarvis in her face. She is staring down at the ground and still smoking as Dan continues to speak. "You must know why I'm here right now; Jarvis is a natural athlete with potential to make it to a big-name college or even the NFL with the right guidance. I can help him develop, but it starts with my training camp. It won't cost you a dime, but I desperately need him game ready by the time next season starts," explains Dan with desperation in his voice. "Please, Miss Naomi. Please, I am begging you." Dan starts to get down on his knees which breaks Nae's firm expression and causes her to smile. Dan sees that he is starting to break down her tough disposition. He looks up, and they both simultaneously burst into boisterous laughter. "Please get up. You're embarrassing me, Mr. Dan," Nae says to Dan as she helps him off the pavement. "Look, I hate to be a hard ass, but Jarvis is my baby, my only baby. I don't plan on having anymore, so I protect him at all costs," Nae explains to Dan. "I know it's time to let him do things that he wants to do. But a part of me is just not ready for him to grow up, and this will be, by far, the most grown-up thing that he has ever done. I'm just scared." Dan places his hand gently on her shoulder as he replies, "I understand. Trust me. I have two kids myself, but they will both be there, along with my wife. Oh, and Corey is coming too!" Naomi looks at Dan for reassurance. "Really? They all gonna be there the whole time while Jarvis is there too?" "Yes ma'am. I even included Corey so Jarvis will feel more comfortable. He isn't half the athlete Jarvis is, but I don't mind hosting both boys. Who knows, he may develop too." "Yes, that's his best friend since they were little kids; his homelife isn't very stable. I like this for him," Nae nods while she speaks as if she is trying to convince herself this is a good idea. Arms folded, she takes a deep breath and with her eyes closed, Nae finally relents, "Okay, okay, okay." Dan holds his arms out. "Thank you, Miss Naomi. I promise to make him the best player the Tigers have ever seen," he says as he embraces her small frame. Her arms remain folded as Dan rocks with her in his arms. Nae suddenly pulls away from Dan's firm hug, drops her cigarette, grabs Dan's arms, and gets in so close to his face he can feel her breath. "You better not let nothing happen to my baby, or me and my family will be at your front door. That's my word!" Dan had a slight moment of fear at her threat. For one, her family may be tough and secondly, his intentions were very disingenuous. Dan just stares speechless at Nae as she suddenly cracks a small smile that turns into the sweetest laughter. Dan pretends to wipe sweat off his forehead as he too laughs with Nae. "I will protect him as if he is one of my own children, Miss Naomi. All my boys are my kids while they are with me," Dan assures Nae. Through her laughter, Nae says, "Please call me Nae, Mr. Dan." Dan grins and says, "Only if you call me Dan, Nae!" "Okay

Dan, you take care of my baby, and we got us a deal." "But just promise me you have him back to me with a little summer left over; he usually spends time with my relatives down in North Carolina. They depend on his help around their property."

Dan assures Nae that the training camp is only four weeks, and there will be plenty of time left for whatever he wants to do before preseason kicks off in August. "Well Dan, you done killed my whole damn break," Nae scoffs as she starts towards the door of the hospital. "I gotta get back, but it's nice to finally meet you; I hope Jarvis accomplishes all that you promise he will!" "We're gonna damn sure try, Nae. You have a good night darling. Take care," says Dan as he starts across the parking lot to his car. Dan thinks to himself how someone looking, from a distance, may assume that Dan and Nae were old friends who had known one another for years. But here they arere, strangers meeting for the first time. In just ten short minutes, Dan had taken a guarded, apprehensive mother, overprotecting of her only child, into a trusted ally. Dan hysterically bursts into the only sincere laugh of the last frenzied twenty-four hours as he pulls out of the hospital parking lot. Dan could not believe his good fortune and what he had just pulled off. A tiny part of him feels guilty for deceiving Nae; he actually likes her, but that feeling soon subsides as he realizes that he likes Jarvis more. The night air blows freely through Dan's hair as he races home hoping for a bit of rest before classes in a few hours. He is not required to be there for any reason, but his house is usually very active and noisy with his kids home for the summer, and the office is welcomed peace.

Dan enters the back door quietly and gently closes it shut, again so, not to disrupt the light sleepers in his home. Dan tiptoes through the dimly lit kitchen. Only a light above the stove guides his subtle steps. Suddenly, a soft voice resonates from the darkest corner of the kitchen table. "Where have you been?" Dan is startled to a near heart attack as he grabs his chest. "Oh my God, Mary. You scared the crap out of me. What are you doing up?" Dan can hardly catch his breath. "I've been up worried about you. You've been leaving the house in the middle of the night lately, and I want to know what you've been doing during these hours of the morning," Dan's wife says, fully ignoring that he is almost in a cardiac arrest. "Taking care of some team business." Dan's short and emotionless in his response as he flops down in the kitchen chair across from where she is seated. "At 3:00 a.m.? Bullshit." Mary's tone is sharp and intense. Dan quickly turns towards her, shocked at her language. No one in the Butler household curses, almost never, so Dan knows that his wife must be very upset at his actions. "Look Mary, I assure you,, everything that I have been doing over the past week has been completely related to the football program. May the good Lord strike me dead right here, right now," Dan explains. Mary looks Dan directly in his eyes as she says, "You swear?" "Yes Mary, I swear. Now let's get some sleep. I want to get a few good hours before work tomorrow." Mary hangs her head as if she questions his explanation, but with no way to disprove the empty account of his whereabouts, she decides this battle isn't worth fighting. Mary's tone changes, "Okay, let's go to bed. I'm tired too. Do you want me to fix you anything to eat?" "No, I'm fine for now. I just want to sleep." Dan gets up from the table, and without even making eye contact with Mary, Dan says, "Tell Michael and Sarah to get the old air mattress out of the shed and clean it off real good. I need it by Sunday." "For what?" Mary's voice is weak and defeated. Dan coarsely replies to Mary's annoying line of questioning, "We're going to have two this summer instead of one. Good night, Mary." Overcome with emotion, a teary-eyed Mary remains seated in the dark while Dan disappears down the hallway.

Dan sleeps without waking up once until 1:00 p.m. the next afternoon. He could not believe that he slept so long into the day, so he just decides to skip classes and head over for practice. Dan arrives on the practice field around 4:00 p.m. and heads straight over to Rick who has already started conducting drills for the evening. Dan stands directly next to Rick with his arms folded, neither of them taking their eyes off the players. "Sorry I've been a bit distant lately, but I had to get a few things lined up for this coming season," Dan speaks in a low, even tone to Rick. "Oh yeah?" replies Rick, genuinely interested in Dan's explanation. "Anything I need to know about? Do you need help with anything?" "Nope, it's all taken care of. This just might be the best season yet." Dan gives a slight grin but remains vague. "Okay, well I will say this, these kids are coming along well. I think we're gonna be okay Coach," Rick echoes the same sentiment. "I need a favor Rick. It's a big one, but I think it's time; I think you can handle it. You in?" "Sure Coach, anything you need. What is it?" asks Rick. "I need you to run the summer training program. I'm going to be working intensively with my two recruits, Jarvis, and Corey. They are too raw and require a rigid regimen to get them in shape." Rick turns to Dan with an astonished look on his face. "Corey? Why him Coach? He's one of the worst out here!" Dan, without skipping a beat, replies, "They were a package. Had to take the dud to get the star." Rick, seemingly pleased with Dan's reasoning, replies, "Oh okay, I guess that makes sense." "Well?" Dan is still waiting for Rick to respond to his original request. "Of course, Dan; it's not like I have anything important going on." "Good," replies Dan. "I appreciate you, Rick; you're a good man. This is for you." Dan reaches into his pocket and retrieves an envelope; he hands it to Rick. "What's this Coach?" "Just a little something to get you through the summer." Rick cracks open the envelope to see what seems like a never-ending supply of crisp one-hundred-dollar bills. "Coach, you don't have to do this. I'd train these guys without this." "I know you would; that's why I'm giving it to you," Dan says with an accomplished smirk on his face. Rick whispers, "How much is this Coach?" "It's nothing. About three thousand dollars, I think." "Wow, thanks Coach. This means a lot, seriously, thank you!" Rick wraps his left arm around Dan's shoulder. "Yeah, yeah, no problem. Don't spend it all on beer and burgers," Dan smiles in Rick's direction. "You know me too well Coach," Rick bellows out as he stuffs the cash into his front pants pocket. Jarvis can be seen in the distance headed towards the two men with the biggest smile on his face. Dan thought to himself in that moment, all is right in the world. He crushed every obstacle in his path. He had effectively persuaded Jackie, Nae, Jay, Jarvis, and Corey while simultaneously buying Rick's time and loyalty. Dan feels unstoppable, and there is only one hurdle left, and that is winning Jarvis' affections. Dan could hardly wait to conquer that challenge.

CHAPTER 7

"MEETING THE BUTLERS"

The time has finally come, and Dan is moving frantically from room to room, making sure everything is in place for the boys' arrival. "Have you started dinner yet Mary?" Dan yells from the spare bedroom after checking to make sure all tasks were performed to his approval. She just stares at him without any expression as she watches his frenzied motions from the doorway of the hallway bathroom. It's hard to tell if Mary is just annoyed at how panic-stricken Dan is over these two boys and how strange his behavior is, or if the recent night's conversation is still lingering in her mind. She finally responds after at least five minutes, "It'll get done." Dan stops his motion almost directly in front of her and asks, "Are you okay? You can't still be upset about the other night; there's no way." Mary just turns and walks to the other side of the house into the master bedroom and shuts the door without a word. Dan just ignores her and keeps on moving like he is busy, but in fact, he is doing a lot of nothing. He seems more nervous than he has been in the past when a recruit was invited over for the summer, and it isn't going unnoticed. Dan turns to Sarah and Michael, who are watching music videos on TV. "Michael, are you ready to go get the boys? I spoke to Nae and Jackie;

both boys are being picked up from that apartment address I gave you earlier." "Yes dad. I'm leaving in fifteen minutes. You said 4:00 p.m., right? It's only about thirteen minutes away according to my calculations, and it's 3:20 now," says Michael as he looks down at his digital wristwatch. Sarah turns to Dan and asks, "Why are you being so weird about everything? I've never seen you like this." Michael chimes in, "Yeah dad. What gives?" Dan doesn't even respond to his kids' line of questioning as he pulls a new pair of sneakers from the top shelf of the hallway closet. Sarah mumbles under her breath, "The same damn homeboys come every year. I wonder what's so special about the little dirty hoodlums this time." It's hard to say if Dan is simply ignoring the comments being made by his kids or if he can't hear them, but either way, he is not reacting. Dan looks down at the crispy new white shoes he now has on his feet. Pleased with the way they fit, Dan walks into one of the spare bedrooms and stares admirably into a body-length mirror hanging on the back of the closet door. The Butler kids are bewildered by his behavior but soon go back to watching TV. About ten minutes go by, and Dan walks out of the bedroom, almost prancing, visibly pleased with his appearance. He has on the same type of clothes he always wears, except the entire outfit, from head to toe, is brand new. Dan walks into the kitchen and realizes that Mary has not started cooking and that she probably is not going to cook at this point. He sharply orders Michael to get up and go pick up the boys in his car immediately. He then orders Sarah to take her car and pick up two ten-piece buckets of fried chicken with all the available sides from Kentucky Fried Chicken. He hands her a crispy one-hundred-dollar bill and tells her she can keep the change. Sarah's irritable demeanor instantly turns into elation as she is presented with her father's cash and means of getting her to shut up. Michael witnesses the transaction between Dan and Sarah and suddenly feels slighted as he was not offered any compensation for his assistance as a taxi service. Michael rolls his eyes as he grabs Dan's keys off the kitchen counter and storms out of the back door to retrieve the boys. Michael dares to say anything in contest to his father. Dan seems to be in a good mood and ignoring his kids' verbal cheap shots. But they know well enough that he has a short temper within the Butler household, and there is no need to push their luck.

Nearly forty-five minutes has gone by, and Dan is anxiously pacing the kitchen floor. He periodically looks out of the small kitchen window directly over the sink. He is frantically checking the entire house for anything dusty, dirty, or out of place. On a normal day, without house guests, the Butler home is completely spotless, so Dan's nervousness concerning the condition of the house is unfounded. As soon as it seems that Dan can no longer take the anticipation, a car pulls into the driveway under the carport. Dan gasps with delight, but it's just Sarah with the food. Dan is somewhat disappointed but heads out to help her bring the meals inside. As he approaches the passenger side of Sarah's car, a horn sounds. It's Michael and the boys pulling in right behind Sarah's car! Dan tries to mask his excitement. He immediately stops helping Sarah and orders Michael to do it. "Michael, help your sister bring dinner inside." Dan doesn't even make eye contact with either of his kids as he heads over to greet his house guests. "Well hello boys. Welcome to the Butler home, also known as your training camp for the next four weeks!" The boys exit one of Dan's three cars. It is like slow motion for Dan, watching Jarvis at his house for the first time. Dan can hardly believe how beautiful Jarvis is. Nae had obviously taken him to get a fresh haircut and new clothes to come stay for the month. Dan is so impressed by Jarvis' neat appearance. He has clean new sneakers on, glistening moisturized skin, a neatly pressed outfit, and trimmed nails. And right behind him, little dusty Corey. He looks about as disheveled as he normally looks, except his same old clothes appear to be clean and his unkept hair is combed down a bit. Corey's sneakers are old and worn, he has on mismatched socks, and he desperately needs a belt. Dan gives a look of disgust after giving Corey the up and down once over. The boys don't even pay any attention to Dan as they gawked in astonishment at the house. They can hardly believe this is how Dan lives as their jaws are dropped at the sight of the Butler home. Dan's house has five bedrooms and four bathrooms, and it was completely newly built and designed by Dan about ten years prior. It is a one-level rancher, completely made of brick. The beautiful four thousand square foot home sits on a well-manicured, nearly one-acre, corner lot. The largest lot, and arguably, one of the nicest homes in the entire subdivision. One may wonder how Dan can afford such a home on a teacher/coach's salary alone. Well, Dan's wife inherited a large sum of money when her father died some years back, and he convinced her to sink a large portion of that money into a dream house for the family. Mary reluctantly succumbed to Dan's wishes and has regretted it ever since, as Dan's behavior has gotten more and more strange over the last decade. She never holds her contribution to their lifestyle over his head, as they are the only two people on earth who know how they came to acquire such a seemingly wealthy appearance. Not to mention, Dan also has three cars, a boat, and a garage full of priceless antiques. People often speak about the Butler house in very high regard and constantly complement Dan for obtaining such a fine home. He graciously takes full credit. But it is because of Mary that any of it even exists.

The boys are escorted into the house by Dan as he helps them carry their belongings inside. Dan is always thrilled to show off his beautiful home as he stands pompously, while the boys are in awe over how neat, clean, and enormous the house is. "Well boys, what do you think?" Dan asks in a haughty tone, already knowing what the boys' response will be. "Coach Dan, this is so awesome! I can't believe this is your house," says Corey. Jarvis echoes Corey's sentiments as he say, "Yeah Coach, I mean, I expected your house to be nice, but I never seen a house this nice before." Dan is so full of himself now; he almost forgets to show the boys to their room. "Come on boys, let me show you where you will be staying," Dan calls out to the boys as he heads down a long hallway where the spare bedroom, Dan's office, and a full bathroom are located. The boys shuffle through the kitchen, past Sarah, who is setting the dining room table for dinner. The coach opens the door and ushers the boys inside. "Welp, here's your room for the next four weeks." The boys slowly peek their heads inside and are amazed at how neat and well put together everything is. Dan even placed a brand-new TV and Nintendo video game console on top of the dresser. The boys see this and go berserk! They run in, jumping on the bed. Then, a puzzled Corey asks, "How come there's only one bed? I'm not sleeping next to his pee-in-the-bed ass." Both boys begin to laugh uncontrollably. Dan gently says to Corey, "Well, I usually only have one, but since there are two of you this time, your bed is on the floor Corey. It was the best I could do on a short notice." The boys both look to the left side of the bed simultaneously to see a twin-sized blow-up mattress neatly tucked beside the full-sized bed. Corey stares at the bed for about ten seconds and then says,

"Better than what I have at home with my little brothers." The coach smiles with relief, as he doesn't want Corey to feel slighted by the situation, though he honestly doesn't care either way. The boys ask if they could please play the video game since neither had one at home to play. Just as Dan is about to relent, Sarah pops in says, "Time for dinner guys." Dan stops Sarah before she walks back to the kitchen. "Where are my manners? Jarvis and Corey, this is my daughter, Sarah. Sarah, this is Jarvis and Corey, my two star recruits this year." Sarah smiles and waves. "Come on fellas. Dinner is getting cold. I bet you boys are hungry! We have some mashed potatoes, mac and cheese, green beans, biscuits, sweet tea, and best of all, FRIED CHICKEN!" Sarah yells with extra emphasis. "Y'all look like you love some fried chicken. There's plenty. Eat as much as you want," Sarah says in a sarcastic but high-pitched, excited voice. The boys reciprocate her enthusiasm by responding with the same high-pitched tone, "Yeah, we love fried chicken." They do not realize that she is making a mockery of them and stereotyping Black people eating fried chicken. Dan shoots Sarah a cold stare as he instructs the boys to wash up in the hallway bathroom and come to dinner. Sarah knows she could get away with these types of actions while the recruits are around because Dan would be preoccupied and pay very little attention to his family during this time.

Thank goodness Dan put aside a plate for Mary; the boys obviously brought their appetites as additional guests. There is no chicken and almost no sides left after the boys demolished the meal that Dan purchased for everyone. Jarvis and Corey had about five pieces each along with two biscuits and huge helpings of sides. They almost looked sick as Dan gazes with adornment at the boy's contentment with the meal. Sarah looks at them with disgust as she began to clean up the mess. Michael seems indifferent to the boys as he lazily helps Sarah tidy the kitchen for five minutes or so, then quietly disappears into his room. Dan laughs to himself at the sight of the boys leaning into one another, bellies so full they could hardly move. "Now boys," Dan speaks in a firm voice, "you can't eat like this every day; you won't be able to perform at the highest level if you don't exercise some self-control. It's not gentleman-like to eat the way you all just did. We gotta work on this!" Both boys attempt to straighten up after the coach makes his statement. "Yes sir!" "Now you boys help Sarah take the trash out and clean this kitchen up; we can worry about the video game tomorrow night if you practice hard." The boys slowly get up and start collecting the accumulated trash as Dan closely monitors their movements, still pleased with how much they enjoyed such a small gesture. Dan had hardly even noticed that Mary had not come out to eat anything until he saw her out of the right corner of his eye quietly walking into the kitchen. "And this boys, is my beautiful wife. Say hello to Mrs. Butler," Dan announces rather loudly. The boys wave and politely say, "Hello Mrs. Butler" as they continue to assist Sarah with the kitchen cleaning duties. Mary does not acknowledge anyone in her presence except Sarah as she kisses her on the forehead while she is washing dishes. Dan lets her know that he has saved her a plate and it is in the oven. She nods, grabs the plate, and disappears back out of the kitchen with her food and a diet soda. Dan, nor the boys, seem to be concerned with Mary's overtly cold behavior as they carry on with their tasks. With the kitchen just about done and now looking more like it did before the feast, Dan directs the boys to clean up and get ready for bed. Dan follows behind and shows them where towels and washcloths are kept and where to put dirty laundry when they are finished. Both boys peep back into the kitchen and say goodnight to Sarah. She smiles and gives a little wave as the boys head down the hall.

Dan's mind races as he stands in the doorway of the spare bedroom, watching Jarvis sleep. A part of him wants to quietly awaken Jarvis from his deep sleep, carry him into his office, and …. but he can't, not yet. Dan had decided early on that he would use a subtle approach, since he has most of the summer to execute his plan and time is needed for a kid like Jarvis. Jarvis, unlike most of the other boys Dan has "mentored," has good parents who care about him. He must ease into the grooming process and present himself as an ally and trusted friend to Jarvis. Dan figures he will start off by basically pushing the boys hard with practice during the day, especially with watchful eyes around. But at night, he will find ways to spoil Jarvis. Making sure that he gets whatever food he likes, staying up to watch TV and play video games, even possibly taking the boys to a theme park or the movies. Just a bunch of small gestures to give the impression that he is a cool friend with fatherly tendencies. These actions will surely soften any kid from a humble environment. Dan's only problem would be Corey. What to do with him while fawning over Jarvis? Dan figures he will keep him busy with various household tasks, even during periods of practice. Dan will make Corey execute yardwork, organizing his shed, various cleaning duties, anything that his wife and kids normally do to keep the house in order will soon become Corey's responsibility. This will all be under the rouse of teaching him structure and discipline. *Yes, this is what I will do*, thought Dan as he watches the boys, mostly Jarvis, sleep. The thought of it all gets Dan extremely excited, in more ways than one. He decides to retire to his office for a release and a good night's rest. Dan is certain tomorrow will be the start of the best summer he has ever experienced!

Dan is startled by his 5:45 a.m. alarm sounding on this digital clock sitting on his office desk. The sun is just starting to rise as he stumbles to stop the annoying chime before it awakens anyone else in the house. Dan prefers to be the first one up in his household no matter what. There is no real benefit to this other than having total control over everything in his life. Thank goodness the door to his office was closed and locked, as Dan soon realizes that his pants are off and boxers around his ankles. He smiles as he pulls up his underwear and pants, thinking that he must've had a great night. He goes to the other side of the house, into the master bedroom where he assumes Mary is probably asleep. He tiptoes in, attempting not to wake her up, as he wants to take a quick shower and get ready before getting Jarvis and Corey up. Mary quickly turns to Dan as he is about to enter the bathroom. "So nice of you to make an appearance on this side of the world, Mr. Butler," she snidely remarks in a soft but condescending tone. Dan stops in his tracks, "Good morning, Mary, darling," he returns, his remarks in the same tone but with a hint of sarcasm. "I just want to get a quick shower before I awake the boys for training. Are you feeling okay this morning, my love?" Mary has picked up on Dan's sarcasm, as he almost never refers to her with endearing pet names. Dan, completely naked at this point before he enters the bathroom, asks Mary if she wants some sausage for breakfast. This is his long-time subliminal way of asking if she wants a morning quickie, which is all she can expect from Dan these days. Dan is notoriously detached and void of any semblance of passion. They stare at one another for about ten seconds as Dan waits for Mary's response, knowing well enough that he could care less and hopes that she says no. She finally rolls her eyes, without any response and flops back down in the bed and pulls the covers over her head. This is surely a "no," and Dan is relieved, as he shows no reaction and heads into the bathroom to start his day. Mary knows that this is likely the last opportunity she will have for a meaningful conversation with her husband until the boys leave. She quietly weeps into her pillow as she has done a hundred times, wishing that Dan were a more loving man. Reality had set in for Mary long ago that Dan will never ever be that man. But vows were taken, and Mary knows that she will suffer in silence until one of them dies. If not for the love of her kids, Mary would probably commit suicide, as she would have nothing to live for. Taking care of Dan has become a chore that has no foreseeable return on investment. Divorce is not an option within her family structure, and she couldn't imagine putting the kids through such an ordeal. Dan emerges from the steamy shower with new underclothes, freshly shaved, and hair neatly combed into place. He heads to the closet to get one of his dry-cleaned outfits for the day. As he spots the garments he wants to wear, a polyester blend polo-style short sleeved shirt and a heavily creased, beige pair of Coach's shorts that he has owned and worn for at least five years but still appear new. Dan pauses while reaching for the garments and thinks to himself that Mary is honestly one of his most trusted and important allies. He must try to always protect her, for she is the glue to everything that Dan maintains. His household, his children, finances, and overall lifestyle. He knows sometimes he will need to toss her a bone to keep her unwavering dedication to him, and now is one of those times. He gives a long sigh, turns, and walks out of the closet towards the bed where Mary is sitting up watching the morning news. She has managed to pull herself together a bit since her emotional breakdown, but it is evident that she has been crying. Dan sits down beside her as he says, "Mary, I just want to apologize if I seem brief and hurt your feelings in any way; it is never my intention to do that. I truly love you and the kids more than anything in this world, but I am passionate about the game of football. I am also passionate about making sure that I turn my players into good men, like we have done with our son. Most of these kids don't have fathers, and I am the closest thing they will ever get to father; it is my duty and a privilege to help our community by creating well-rounded citizens for Heritage Park and beyond. My calling is much bigger than you think; it can actually affect the entire world Mary, but none of it is remotely possible without you. I NEED YOU!" Dan gives a gentle smile as he looks at Mary, and she soon returns a small smirk back at him. They laugh as he pulls her towards him and kisses her on the forehead. "I love you mama." That is something he used to say to her years ago while they were courting. He stands up and continues to get ready for practice with the boys. Out of Mary's view, Dan's smile quickly turns sullen. Dan knows that this one small act could carry him through the entire summer without another inharmonious word from his wife. Though Dan hates that he must perform such ridiculous acts to maintain peace in his life, he also understands how necessary it is. There is absolutely no genuine emotion involved; it is all a chess game to Dan, and he must absolutely always win. Dan is now fully dressed and looking very sharp, even by his own high standards. He gives a little twirl and asks Mary how he looks. She smiles and replies, "Very handsome, Mr. Butler. Handsome indeed." Dan heads towards the doorway and stops, turns to Mary. She looks as if she is anticipating more warm words from Dan. He gently says, "Mary, please don't forget lunch for me and the boys around noon. We have a long day planned, and the sun will be relentless today. Thanks!" Mary replies, "Sure thing, Mr.

Butler." Dan smiles and turns to walk out; he knows he has her, just like he has everyone else in his life. Everyone has a quantifiable price, whether emotional or financial. Dan gladly pays suggested retail without negotiation to maintain control of his lifestyle. CHECKMATE!

CHAPTER 8

"OBVIOUS INTERFERENCE"

By now it is almost 8:00 a.m., and the sun is already brutal and seems to be at least 90 degrees in the shade. The boys are sitting under the covered patio behind the Butler home waiting for Dan to appear and start the training. They are excited but also tired from the previous night's activities. They both are slumped over and snuggly laying on the beautiful outdoor furniture that is a perfect complement to every part of the Butler home. The patio furniture almost looks as if it could belong indoors. A vibrant mash of blue and green palm tree pattern adorns the plush cushions that sit on top of the authentic tropical rattan. Thick, frosted glass tabletops are sprinkled in between the seating arrangements thoughtfully, as if to offer the perfect guest accommodation. Dan also recently had an outdoor BBQ pit added as part of the patio, equipped with a refrigerator and drink bar. The area itself is large, and the furniture could probably seat a minimum of twelve people comfortably. The patio overlooks a sprawling, manicured yard that could rival any golf course putting green. Evenly height shrubs, maybe five feet, line the street side of the property and provide a bit of privacy from passing traffic. The scene in its entirety just seems perfect for entertaining. Jarvis and Corey are too tired to appreciate how stunning this setting truly is, as they appear to be dozing off.

The boys seem to be immersed in their morning nap when Mary bursts through the sliding glass door with a tray full of food and drinks. She is jubilant and joyful as she approaches the boys with a breakfast of bacon, toast, scrambled eggs, fresh strawberries, jelly, and orange juice. "Good morning boys. Time for breakfast. Gotta get you ready for this training Coach Butler has lined up for you!" The last thing the boys want is food, but they do not want to be rude, as Mary has taken her time to prepare a meal for them. She places the tray down between them as they struggle to get up from their morning nap. "Thank you, Mrs. Butler," the boys speak in unison, appreciating the gesture that Mary has provided them. Once the boys see how beautifully displayed the spread is, they begin to devour the meal as if all the food they had stuffed down the night before has been forgotten. The boys nor Mary realize that Dan is watching the entire interaction from the open sliding glass door, his arms crossed and an enormously pleased smile on his face. All is well in the Butler home, and Dan couldn't be any more elated at the turn of events in the last twenty-four hours. Mary seems to be taking a more nurturing role with boys, as she gently attends to them while they gorge on the meal she has prepared. The boys can hardly believe their good fortune with the treatment bestowed upon them by Coach Dan and his family. It almost seems like a dream. Mary happens to glance over and notice Dan smiling. She smiles back as Dan places his finger over his lips to signal to Mary not to alert the boys to his presence. She nods as she steadily cleans up behind Jarvis and Corey. Corey, with a mouth full of food, quietly comments to Jarvis that this is probably the best food he has eaten in his whole life. Mary, pretending not to pay attention, heard this, and it broke her heart. This is a simple meal by her estimation, something she merely threw together so the boys would not be hungry during practice. Her kids get these types of meals all the time and probably take it for granted. But here is Corey and Jarvis, cherishing every bite. At that very moment, Mary decides that she will take a more nurturing and motherly role with these two, something she had never done before with the summer recruits. Dan observes this interaction as it is taking place. On the one hand, he loves that his wife is taking such an active role in making sure the boys are cared for. But on the other hand, he must maintain distance between both worlds. He does not want to create a situation where the boys trust Mary enough to confide in her. Just as Mary is about to sit and chat with the two, Dan pops out of the sliding door, "Morning boys! How is breakfast?" Dan is loud enough to disrupt any feelings that are being exchanged between Mary and the boys at that moment. The boys look up excitedly at Dan. "It's so good," says Jarvis, and Corey just nods in approval as his mouth is too full to verbally reply. "Well hurry up. Training starts in three minutes. We are going to start with stretching and conditioning." "Yes sir." The boys hurry and wipe their faces and hands. Jarvis starts to help Mary clean up, and Dan firmly delivers instructions to leave the mess for Mary. This sudden sharpness in his tone startles Mary and the boys. They all turn and gaze in Dan's direction as if to ask, "Why so harsh?" Dan clears his throat and takes a deep sigh after the realization that his tone may have come off a bit callous. "Excuse me, I just need the boys to come along with me so we can get started. Come on boys." Dan turns and walks in the direction of the grassy lawn without even batting an eye at Mary. Unfazed, she continues to clean as the boys hop up and scurry behind the coach, Corey still chewing.

Dan opens a small, dusty door on the back side of his large shed. The boys look curious, yet cautiously into the dark opening. "Grab those cones and set them up along that side of the yard." Dan points to the side closest to the street. Flies, gnats, and yellow jackets all swarm in and out of the door where the cones are located. Both boys look reluctant as they slowly walk towards the shed door. The cones, and everything in that portion of the shed, are covered in cobwebs, and both Jarvis and Corey are too petrified to move any further. "NOW!" yells Dan. The boys move quickly into the filthy, narrow space. They run inside and quickly back out with the cones as Dan requested. Dan wants to laugh at how frightened they are but keeps a rigid look on his face while the boys do exactly what he has instructed. Any tell of emotion from Dan is always well hidden behind the aviator shades that he frequently wears. Dan watches the boys from a distance as they set up the cones on the opposite side of the yard. It is extremely hot by now, and any movement in the humid Virginia sun will surely cause sweat. Corey and Jarvis are both drenched while carrying out Dan's orders, and it does not go unnoticed by him. Jarvis' skin is glistening in the sun, as it has turned a beautiful golden shade of brown. The sunlight mixed with sweat makes Jarvis' skin, body, and hair almost unbearable to Dan as he continues to quietly observe from across the yard. In that moment, he wants to touch Jarvis, badly, but discipline will always be one of Dan's greatest strengths. Though Dan's actions can come off as extreme to the average person, he sees no malice in what he does. One thing Dan prides himself on is the fact that he makes a conscious effort to never ever penetrate his victims. He does anything you can possibly think of sexually besides that, but he feels that this, in his own twisted logic, is a way of carrying out a reciprocal pleasured act. Dan has engaged in full blown acts in the past where he entered his victims but found that it usually broke their spirits and made them unable to perform during the season, post assault. Dan, with his delusional mindset, thinks that these boys actually enjoy these acts that he has mentally and physically groomed them to take part in. He also threatens them after these acts have taken place. Telling them that he will lie if they tell anyone and say they are making it up. Usually following up his threats with harsh demeaning words like, "Who would believe some poor Black trash like you over me?" Dan also tells them they will have no opportunity to play football without his help; if they are smart, they should keep quiet. And lastly, he will inform their families that they are in fact homosexuals and that it was them that tried to come on to him. He will then expose this lie to the entire community as well. Any of these things could be devastating to a young Black kid in the 1980s. Without college or sports, these kids felt as if they had no other choice but compliance. They do as they are told but always end up suffering in silence, while Dan feels as though he has done them a favor.

Dan is patient and has resolved to wait for the exact right time to carry out his dubious intentions. Jarvis has on a tight pair of jeans that have obviously been repurposed and cut into shorts. They show off his long muscular legs. Jarvis is also sporting a new white tank top that his mom purchased for the stay with the Butlers. Jarvis lifts his shirt to wipe the sweat from his face. This reveals just a light strip of hair from his navel, all the way up his thin chiseled stomach, to the bottom of his toned chest. The band of his underwear peeks over the top of his jean shorts, the sweat beading and running all over his body. Dan can hardly contain himself at the sight of it all. Just when Dan thinks that it can't get any better, he comes up with an idea.

"Hey boys, do those stretches that we used to do before practice." The boys nod and start the stretching exercises they learned just a few short weeks ago. By now, both boys are bending and before long, they are on the ground, legs wide and leaned over. Dan catches a glimpse of Jarvis' crotch and begins to daydream lustful thoughts. He starts to let his imagination get the best of him when suddenly, Corey yells, "What now Coach?" Dan snaps out of his daze and notices that both boys are no longer in the distance and now nearly in front of him. They are both just standing and waiting for further instruction. Dan straightens up, regains his composure, and quickly turns to walk in the direction of the cones so his excitement is not noticeable. Jarvis, as always, is oblivious to Dan's strange behavior, but for some reason, Corey seems to take notice. Corey tries to ignore what he thinks he saw and shrugs it off as effects from the heat. Because he is unsure, Corey decides not to alert Jarvis of his thoughts. Dan slowly walks across the yard to give himself time to fix his hair and clothes. He then walks the cones one by one in a particular pattern. Corey and Jarvis just look puzzled while Dan carries out his task. Once complete, Dan takes a silver whistle hanging around his neck and blows it as loudly as possible while signaling for the boys to come in his direction. They run over and stand directly in front of Dan, curious about what the coach has planned for them. Dan instructs them to first run the perimeter of the yard four times, about the distance of a mile. He tells them that he will start his stopwatch and time them to test their endurance. Then once they are done, he will have them run drills. The boys aren't excited about all that running in the hot sun but know that they must do as the coach insists. They both line up and get ready for the coach's start whistle. "Ready, set, go! The boys take off running around Dan's sprawling backyard. There is a faint dirt path where they are running, likely made by past recruits carrying out the same routine. Dan realizes that he may have dodged a bullet by allowing his emotions to get the best of him earlier. He vows at that moment to not let it happen again, as he is not used to having two students in his home versus usually only having one. He puts little stock into Corey, though, and thinks that he will not be able to catch on to his interactions with Jarvis. Full of himself, Dan strongly believes that he can carry out his intentions with both boys present.

Dan and the boys rest under the patio after the intense workout. Mary brought out water and fruit for the boys. Jarvis and Corey have been resting for more than ten minutes and still can't seem to catch their breath. Mary whispers to Dan that lunch is almost ready and maybe he can just let them relax for another twenty minutes or so until it is done. He nods in agreement. Dan relays this message to the boys but also lets them know that after lunch, they will repeat the same activity, one mile timed and speed drills with cones. Corey and Jarvis look at each other in disbelief that they will have to continue such an intense work out in the heat. It is nearly one hundred degrees, and neither of them thinks they can go on. Corey, scared to speak up, nudges Jarvis into speaking up for the both of them. Jarvis gathers himself and clears his throat to get Dan's attention. "Ummm, Coach Dan, don't you think it's a bit hot out today to do so much running? I mean, we could literally die out here, heat stroke or something like that." Jarvis sounds sincere and honestly concerned with his questioning. Dan, retorts without hesitation, "I thought about that Jarvis, and I was only going to make you boys run this drill one more time seeing as how out of shape you both are. But since you opened your mouth, let's make it two more times. I will allow you to rest for ten minutes in between. I will make you both run all day, every day until you get this time down. I don't care if you don't touch a single football all summer. Now go get washed up for lunch." Corey shoots Jarvis the glare of death as they slowly head for sliding glass door. Jarvis can be heard mumbling, "But you're the slow one. How can you be mad at me?" Dan has no intention of making them run as much as he just threatened. He just wants to come off as the bad guy for a bit, and then when he relaxes his rules, it will cause Jarvis to trust him even more. By the time all of this takes place, he will have Corey swamped with household chores and out of Dan and Jarvis' sight. But for the rest of this week, hard work. Dan's plan is not in full swing.

One week of nonstop, grueling running in the humid Virginia heat has undoubtedly taken its toll on the boys. They both look visibly thinner, and Corey has thrown up at least three times. This is a combination of the sun, his extreme appetite, and the overexertion of his weak body over the past five days. But one can give Corey the benefit of the doubt, as he has cut his time by almost half over the course of the week. It is now Saturday morning, and Dan figures he will lighten up on the boys a bit seeing as they have carried out the main task that he requested. He is proud of how well they are progressing. But Dan has his own goals to work on, and it just won't wait any longer. Dan feels like it is time to start separating the two boys, so he has some chores arranged for Corey to carry out while he works one-on-one with Jarvis. He will disguise his intentions by stating that Jarvis will join him and help finish up any assigned chores later, but he needs specialized training in the quarterback position. This does not require Corey's presence. Dan has thought this through thoroughly while the boys are eating their breakfast. Just as they are about to finish, Dan hits them with his plan. "Corey,

I'm going to get you to wash my car today. No rain in the forecast for the next few days, so I want her looking good. Think you can handle that for me? Few bucks in it for you if you do a good job." Corey excitedly nods. "Sure Coach!" "Thank you, Corey," says Dan. "I need to work with Jarvis on some passing drills, so he can be starting QB this upcoming season. I have high expectations for him in that position. Gonna take hard work, though. Can I count on you, Jarvis?" "I will promise you I will try my best Coach," Jarvis replies. "Perfect, let me pull the car around Corey. I will get you all the supplies that you need. I normally make my son do this, but I think you can handle it." Dan places his hand on Corey's shoulder as he stands up. Corey nods and with a big smile, hops up to await his job. He is just happy to not be running on this day. Dan pulls his car under the carport, shows Corey where the water hose and supplies are, and leaves him to complete the task. Given Corey's level of laziness and lack of athletic ability, he figures he should have at least two hours with Jarvis on the patio. This time will be spent talking again, just as he had done at school that day but more intense. Michael is off with a couple of friends and Sarah is working her summer job. Mary volunteers two Saturdays a month at a women's shelter in the city. She teaches them administrative skills like using the phone, typing, and filing documents. This leaves just Dan and the boys home alone for about three or four hours until Mary is back. Dan plans to make good use of this time. Corey will be in the distance and have visibility of the patio but should be well occupied with Dan's car.

Corey starts spraying the car down while Dan is headed back over to the patio where Jarvis is relaxing. He is laying down flat on his back, hands behind his head, both feet planted on the cement but legs open. What a sight for Dan to be welcomed to, but he resists temptation and simply taps him on the elbow. "Hey, you, get up." Jarvis opens his eyes as if Dan were gone for an hour with Corey; it was only about ten minutes. Jarvis sits up while Dan plops down on the cushion next to him. Dan starts the conversation, "What's up? Whatcha got on your mind?" Jarvis gives a nervous smile as he replies, "Nothing much Coach. I just want to make a good impression with this opportunity you're giving me. I really appreciate it, especially the meals." Dan chuckles at Jarvis' response. "You are certainly welcome young man." Jarvis looks down at his hands. "Thank you looking out for Corey too. I know you only did it for me, but he really needed this, more than I did honestly. His home life is crazy; he has a bunch of brothers and sisters and what not. Plus—" Jarvis pauses for a spell, "I feel like I owe him." "Why is that?" Dan questions Jarvis. Jarvis takes a deep breath before replying, "Coach, I got something I want to get something off my chest, and you're the only person I feel like I can trust, other than Corey. But I can't tell him this. Promise me we will keep it between us. Please?" Jarvis pleads for Dan's discretion in this matter. "Of course, Jarvis. What is it? It can't be that bad. You're such a good kid." Dan can hardly wait to see what juicy secret Jarvis is holding. "Well, remember when I told you about that girl that I was messing around with that day when we were at school?" Jarvis' head hangs lower and lower with every word. "Yes, I do, but what about it?" Dan is now on the edge of his seat. "Everything I said really happened, even more actually, but I lied about the girl." Dan is confused, now wondering why Jarvis is making such a big deal about this. "I don't understand Jarvis. Well, if it wasn't Janice, I think you said her name was, then who was it?" Jarvis mumbles so low, Dan can barely hear him. "Her name is Jackie." Dan is still confused, "Did you say Jackie? Who is

Jackie? I don't understand," Dan asks with a puzzled look on his face. Jarvis looked up with his eyes just about to water, ashamed, he said, "It's Corey's mom. I used to meet her in the alley after school while Corey was babysitting, and his dad was at work." Dan is completely astonished but tries not to show it. "Wow, well I wasn't expecting that, not that I'm judging you, Jarvis." Jarvis responds, "Yeah, I'm not proud, but every time I was at their apartment, she would always be wearing these robes. And when no one was paying attention, she would open it so I could see her naked body. After a while, I would go in her room when no one was looking and touching her breasts. Soon after that, we made plans to meet. At first, it was just her jerking me off, but eventually, it turned into her sucking. I enjoyed it for a few months, I guess, but I started feeling so guilty, so I cut it off. Corey has been my best friend since we were little. I couldn't keep betraying him like that. I just stopped showing up maybe a couple of months ago. I just couldn't do it anymore Coach." Dan still can't believe the information that he just took in and is struggling to give a meaningful response. He is torn between feeling jealousy and elation at the thought of it all. Dan settles his discombobulated mind on being grateful that Jarvis has been sexualized by another adult already. In Dan's twisted mind, this will make Jarvis easily relent to his advances. Besides, Dan has invested too much effort at this point; he must see his plan through. Finally, after about two minutes of silence, Dan says, "Well Jarvis, you're a young man, and young men have needs. I can't say that I wouldn't have done the same thing if I was in your shoes. As a matter of fact, I know for a fact, a fourteen-year-old me would've done exactly what you did. Hell, at my age now, I may have done it." Dan tries to lighten the mood by making a joke. "By the way, I saw them big ol' titties through that robe when I went to talk to her that day. I know what you mean!" Dan and Jarvis both let out a hearty laugh, so much so that Corey stops washing the car and looks over at the two. They realize how loud they are and immediately tone down their laughter. Corey gazes for a second or two and then resumes his activity. Jarvis now looks as if a one-hundred-pound weight has been lifted off his chest. "Thanks for listening Coach; it was really eating me up." "No problem, Jarvis; you can tell me anything. I am here for you." Dan stands up and positions himself behind Jarvis. Dan begins to caress Jarvis' shoulders in a circular massage type motion. Jarvis welcomes the coach's firm hands on his back and shoulders after all the exercise they have done over the past week. Jarvis lets out a little moan. "Wow, thanks Coach. I really need this; my body has been killing me." Dan is excited again, but not sure what the next move should be, he chooses to just keep rubbing Jarvis' back, arms, and shoulders. Jarvis is faced away from Dan and cannot see how the coach is reacting, so in his naive mind, this is all innocent. Corey is wiping down the car with a rag when he looks up to see Dan seductively rubbing Jarvis' shoulders. Dan seems to be enjoying the moment too much as Corey can obviously observe Dan's hips thrusting with every motion of his hands, digging deep into Jarvis' flesh. Dan's eyes have begun to roll back as he appears to be in an extremely heightened realm of ecstasy. Corey is not confused this time by what is happening right before his eyes; it would be obvious to even a blind man that this situation is highly inappropriate. Corey is appalled and repulsed by how Dan is behaving with his friend. Neither of them can see Corey behind Dan's car, but he can see everything clearly. Corey is instantly triggered by events from his own past when he sees how Dan is touching Jarvis. Corey suddenly feels dizzy, and his mind starts to wonder back to events that he had long shut out of his mind from fear.

There he was. Corey as a little, curious, and lively seven-year-old boy. He would talk to just about anybody and run the halls of their apartment building like a wild animal. Corey was cute and talkative, which made him loved and protected by his family as well as neighbors. Corey is the oldest sibling and had only two younger brothers at the time. One was four and the other, in diapers, barely walking. Even though they lived in a two-bedroom apartment, there was Corey, his two siblings, Jackie and Milton all stuffed in there together. Corey slept in a room with him and his brothers, rotating between a top and bottom bunk bed. Of course, the baby slept on the bottom, and no one wanted to sleep next to him without him being completely potty trained. So, most nights, Corey would fall asleep on the top bunk alone but usually woke up next to the four-year-old. Conditions were already cramped when Corey's uncle, Marvin, came to stay with them. Marvin was an eighteen-year-old high school dropout who couldn't stay out of trouble. He was Milton's youngest brother, the baby of the family. Milton's mother could no longer control Marvin and was at her wit's end when she put him out on the street with nowhere to go. When word got back to Milton that his brother was sleeping outside in the cold, he picked him up and brought him home to stay with them. Corey had seen Uncle Marvin many times at family events or random visits to the apartment. It was always brief encounters without much more than a dap and a few empty words exchanged. Marvin was not the most handsome guy on earth, but what he lacked in looks, he made up in muscles. Marvin is tall, brown-skinned with a naturally muscular build. His personality is jovial, as he seems to have a constant dimpled smile, exposing a shiny gold tooth on the side of his perfect white teeth. Marvin slept on the sofa in the living room which was the only unoccupied space for sleeping in the whole apartment. Corey and Marvin's paths usually only crossed during daylight hours, but this night was different. Corey was fast asleep but suddenly awakened by someone tugging on his favorite little night shirt. Corey gasped loudly with fear, unsure if he was still asleep and dreaming while this was occurring. Corey's little eyelids extend as widely as possible to try and see what was grabbing him in the blackness of night. He could barely make out the dark shadowy figure in front of him when he heard a whisper, "Shhhhh, it's me, Uncle Marvin. Don't be scared. I got some candy in here if you want it; we can watch wrestling too." Wiping the crust from his tired eyes, he shook his head yes and allowed Marvin to help him on to the floor. He grabbed Marvin's hand as they walked to the living room. Marvin sat on the couch, and Corey sat Indian style in front of the TV. Marvin made a noise to get Corey's attention, "Psssst, here." He tossed Corey a little chocolate candy bar, which he caught, opened, and inhaled, all in one swift motion. "Damn, at least say thank you lil nigga," Marvin said jokingly. Everyone, except Corey and Marvin, were asleep, and the only light in the blackness of the entire apartment was from the TV. Corey sat close to the TV so he could hear what was being said. Marvin had the volume down so no one would wake up. A voice could suddenly be heard over the quiet hum of the TV noise. "Come sit up here with your uncle little man," Marvin says in a gentle soothing tone. Corey turns sharply towards his uncle as he is patting the cushion beside him to gesture for Corey to sit next to him. Corey unwittingly obliges by hopping up and bouncing into the spot next to Marvin. At first, they both are just sitting and watching wrestling on the TV. One little guy in a red speedo is getting destroyed by a much bigger guy in a one-piece, leopard print, spandex bathing suit, and calf-high boots. Corey laughs, even though he can't hear what they are saying. A few more minutes go by when Marvin, out of nowhere, grabs Corey's hand and places it on his private. Corey tries to move his hand, but Marvin is very forceful and much stronger than him. Marvin is moving his hips while holding Corey's hand in place. Corey doesn't understand exactly what is happening, but he is certain that it doesn't feel right. Marvin proceeds to unzip his pants and expose his penis. Corey sees Marvin's erect manhood and feels a sharp pain in his stomach brought on by extreme fear. Corey tries pulling his hand back again as he shakes his head and whimpers, "No, no, stop, please." But he is too weak, and Marvin issues a firm threat, "Stop pulling or I'll kill you. You understand? Stop it now! I'll cut your little throat, now grab it!" All Corey can remember is Marvin forcing him to move his small hand up and down for a couple of minutes, Marvin letting out muffled groan, he felt something wet, and it was over. Marvin jumped up and quickly ran to the hallway bathroom. Corey just sat there on the sofa sobbing. His chest was pulsating aggressively, but no noise came out of his mouth as the tears flowed endlessly. Marvin came back with some tissue and wiped Corey's face and hand, trying to nervously cover up what had just happened. "Look, stop it, all this bitch ass crying. You better not say a fucking word, or I'll kill you, Jackie, and your brothers. I'll kill everybody and myself in this motherfucka, so keep your mouth shut. You hear me!" He shook Corey by the shoulders, then picked him up, and walked back to the bedroom where he carelessly threw him onto the top bunk and walked out of the bedroom. Corey sobbed all night in the darkness, scared to move, scared Marvin would come back, scared to tell his parents, and scared Marvin would kill everyone. From this point on, Corey was not the same little boy, and everybody saw it. The light in him died, and no one could understand why. The abuse continued during the six months that Marvin stayed with them. The sexual cruelty escalated, and Corey became numb to it. The talkative little boy who used to smile and laugh was no longer present. A new boy showed up, and he was quiet and withdrawn. He lacked self-confidence and was scared to get undressed, even to take showers. He no longer washed or kept up with hygiene. He became a shell of what he used to be. His parents couldn't understand, so they yelled at him and beat him when he didn't listen to them, not knowing how he had suffered. Corey didn't care; anything was better than what Marvin did to him. Marvin eventually went to prison for armed robbery. Word on the street is Milton was the one who called the cops on him. There was also a rumor around the community that Corey's youngest sibling, a baby girl named Wendy, was actually fathered by Marvin. It is unclear if Milton caught wind of that same rumor but not long after her birth, Marvin disappeared, sentenced to twenty years in a maximum-security facility. Milton never mentioned him again, except this one time when Corey overheard his father say that Marvin was a punk in prison. In other words, he was somebody's bitch, and everybody knew it. When Corey heard this, he was about ten years old and smiled for the first time in three years. He met Jarvis two months later.

Corey shook his head, finally snapping out of his trance-like state. He must've suffered from a panic attack and lost consciousness. Corey had suppressed these memories and fears for years, but here they were, resurfacing after seeing Dan sexually rubbing Jarvis. Corey is determined to protect his friend from the type of agony he suffered. Corey felt as though he was out for hours, but in reality, it is more like a couple minutes because Dan is still grinding his hips and rubbing Jarvis' shoulders, just as he had been doing before Corey passed out. Corey knows he has to do something to interfere with what the Coach is doing, but what? Corey thought hard about how he could interrupt them without letting the coach know why he is doing it. Corey did not want to make things worse for Jarvis. Crouched down behind Dan's car, Corey decides to intervene by spraying water in their direction and apologizing as if it were an accident. It is worth a try, and Corey knows he will likely pay a harsh penalty from Dan, but he is desperate to protect Jarvis. Shaking like a leaf, Corey takes the hose and points it in the direction of the patio where Jarvis and Dan are immersed in their rub-down session, oblivious to the world. Corey shuts his eyes and presses down on the hose lever and sprays both Jarvis and Dan. The bulk of the water hits Dan directly in the face and some gets on Jarvis too. You would think Dan is drowning based off his reaction to the water hitting him. He gasps for air as he throws his sunglasses to the ground and immediately palms his face. Jarvis looks in Corey's direction and angrily yells, "What the hell man?" Just before Jarvis jumps up to chase Corey, Corey yells, "I'm sorry Coach; it was an accident, I swear." Corey starts running once he notices Jarvis barreling towards him full speed, but he is too slow. Jarvis tackles him about as hard as a professional football player. The two roll around on the ground laughing as Dan fixes his hair and clothes. Deep down inside, Dan knows that he needed that interjection because things were starting to get out of hand again, but it did not stop him from being enraged. Once he regains his composure and fixes his appearance, he marches straight over to where the boys are wrestling. With one hand, he picks Corey up by the collar of his shirt and holds his face close to his, lips cinched tight around his big white teeth. Dan delivers a stern message to Corey. "If you ever do something like that again, I will beat you unconscious. You understand me?" Corey smiled, "Yes sir; it'll never happen again. The hose just got away from me when I was cleaning your rims." Dan throws Corey on the ground like a bag of trash. "Now finish cleaning my car. After you're done, I need you to do two miles." Corey isn't even mad; it is all worth it if he can save his best friend from the same bleak fate he had suffered.

Now it is night, and the eventful day had taken a toll on everyone in the Butler household. Sarah had worked all day. Mary volunteered at the women's shelter. Michael went hiking in the mountains with some friends, and the boys ran in the heat all evening. Dan did not do much physical activity, but his blood is still boiling after Corey interrupted his moment with Jarvis. Dan is torn between further torturing Corey or picking up where he left off with Jarvis earlier. He settles on the latter of the two. It isn't super late, maybe 10:00 p.m. or so, but everyone in the Butler home had pretty much retired to their own rooms after dinner. Dan plotted intensively about how to get Jarvis in his study alone tonight. He knows there would be great risk involved with Corey on the floor next to Jarvis, but Dan no longer cared. It is time to make his move and would just have to be very careful. Dan figures it would make sense to wait until about midnight, even later perhaps. This way he can be assured that everyone is asleep. Dan sits, anxiously waiting in his study for the right time to gently awaken Jarvis and coax him into the study. Groggy and unsteady, Dan will be able to have his way with Jarvis, and he probably will not put up much of a fight. *Yes*, Dan thought. This is the perfect idea, so long as Corey doesn't wake up. It is now about 12:30

a.m., and Dan has waited long enough. He tip-toes out of his study into the hallway. He stops in tracks just to have a listen and make sure there is no one awake throughout the house. Not a peep from any corner of the entire house. Perfect! Dan peeps his eye into a small crack in the doorway where the boys are. He then opens the bedroom door halfway so the light from the hallway can delicately cascade into the room, and he can see the boys. They appear to be asleep. Corey is facing the opposite direction of the door, and Dan cannot directly see his face. There doesn't seem to be any movement from either of the boys, so Dan now opens the door just wide enough to fit his body in. He is slow and patiently taking each step, so he does not wake Jarvis up suddenly before he plans to. Dan is now standing directly over Jarvis and just marveling over how peacefully he is sleeping. He almost feels bad about having to wake him up, but he also feels, in a twisted way; he is doing this for both of them to feel good. Dan snaps out of his daze, tenderly pulls the covers off Jarvis, leans down to touch his arm, and … Corey suddenly gives a big stretch and exudes a rather loud yawn. Dan is petrified at the thought of Corey being awake and even more of the thought he will catch him inside the room. He freezes in complete fear. Then Corey sits up but not facing Dan's direction. Dan makes a hasty decision to retreat before Corey sees him. He shuffles backwards out of the bedroom and gently pulls the door so there is still a small crack. Dan then quickly runs into his study, closes, and locks the door. He is sweating profusely, and his heart is beating out of his chest. *Twice in one day*, Dan starts to think that these incidents are more than just coincidence. *But how could dopey, dimwitted Corey catch on to me?* Dan thought. "Maybe I'm being silly. Yes, there is no way any of this is on purpose," Dan quietly says out loud. Dan takes a deep breath, laughs it off, and decides to come up with a better way to occupy Corey. It will have to wait until tomorrow though. Dan is exhausted with his failed efforts and simply wants to sleep at this point. Dan decides to retire to his bed with his wife tonight. He exits his study and heads for the other side of the house. Just as Dan disappears into the darkness, Corey opens the spare bedroom door, looks both ways, smiles, and closes the door and locks it.

It is now Sunday morning, and the boys, Mary, Michael, and Sarah all seem to be well rested and are gathered at the kitchen table for breakfast. Dan, still a bit dejected by the previous day's events, opted to sit on the patio and read the Sunday paper with a cup of coffee. Sarah and Mary seem especially interested in how the boys are coming along and, overall, doting on them excessively. There is lots of laughter and joy while everyone interacts over the amazing meal Mary cooked. The spread includes waffles, scrambled eggs, bacon, sausage, toast, fried apples, and fried potatoes. Both boys, as usual, are eating like it's their last meal. Of course, Jarvis has much better table manners than Corey, and it doesn't go unnoticed. Mary continuously comments on how neat Jarvis presents himself, his good posture, clean appearance, and how helpful he is. Corey is a stark opposite of all the good qualities that Jarvis possesses. Corey doesn't seem to care what anyone thinks about him. He understands well enough that he may never get to eat and live like this again. Soon, it will all be over, and Corey knows that he will have to return to a life where meals were not nearly as extravagant, free time was filled with babysitting, and he had a father with a temper. The Butler home is like a vacation compared to his homelife. Dan finishes his coffee and paper and decides that he will play the "good guy" role for a bit. No running for Jarvis and Corey today; he is going to do some passing drills, something he knows that the boys have been dying to work on. Yes, he will finally break out the football. In Dan's mind, this will have two positive effects. For one, it will allow Dan to truly gauge the boy's abilities and agility and figure out how they will fit onto the team. Secondly, it will relieve some tension after everything that happened the day before. Basically, wiping the slate clean and gaining trust, especially with Corey, who Dan is now suspicious of.

It is another sunny day in Heritage Park but not quite as hot as the weather had been previously. It is 88 degrees, perfect for the activities Dan had planned for the boys that day. After breakfast is done and the boys have finished assisting Mary with a few chores, Dan takes them out to the patio to inform them of the training he has lined up for them. The boys' body language implies that they are expecting more running, and they are not too excited about it. Both Jarvis and Corey file out of the sliding door and plop down on to the patio furniture. All the smiles and laughter at breakfast are now in the past, as the boys appear despondent. They sit as if they are waiting on a death row when suddenly, Dan emerges from the shed with two footballs. The boys light up and excitedly run over to where Dan is. The smiles are back, and both Jarvis and Corey are about as happy as they have ever been since they first arrived at the Butler home. Dan instructs each of the boys to spread out to opposite far corners of the yard so that they can do some passing drills. They follow Dan's directions with animated enthusiasm, running to their perspective spots in the yard. Dan reels back and launches the football in Corey's direction first. He looks as if he is prepared for the pass but ultimately fumbles Dan's perfectly spiraled throw. Dan drops his head and realizes that Corey will need a tremendous amount of work to even justify him riding the bench for the upcoming season. Jarvis bursts out into a laughing fit at

Corey's lack of athletic ability. Dan takes the second football and mirrors the exact same pass to Jarvis. Jarvis impressively leaps in the direction of Dan's pass, which was not thrown with the same accuracy as Corey's pass, and he catches it with one hand. *Wow*, Dan thinks to himself. This kid is a gold mine as he imagines Jarvis playing multiple positions on the football field. Having a player with the athleticism that Jarvis possesses can be a game changer for the Heritage Park football program. Dan backs up to the absolute furthest part of his yard and instructs Jarvis to throw the ball back to him. Dan knows Jarvis has an arm, but he wants to test his accuracy. Jarvis clutches the football, slings his arm back, and effortlessly floats the most beautiful, perfect spiral pass ever in Dan's direction. Dan isn't nearly the athlete he used to be but manages to clutch Jarvis' pass after stumbling and almost losing his balance. Corey is standing back, equally excited about Jarvis' throw and Dan's catch. Corey runs to the middle of the yard, cheering both Dan and Jarvis at the same time. "Oh my God! That was awesome!" Corey yells while shifting his attention back and forth in both directions. Dan smiles, impressed with his own ability to catch the rocket that Jarvis hurled at him. Dan walks over and gives Jarvis a high five. "That was amazing young man." Jarvis is proud of his pass and the congratulations that he has just received from Dan and Corey as well. "Thanks Coach. I can't wait to help the team this season," Jarvis humbly receives his praise. In this instance, Sarah, Mary, and Michael all file onto patio, cheering and clapping as well. Jarvis is now embarrassed by all the commotion but still smiling with his head aimed at his feet. Sarah and Michael walk over in Jarvis' direction, and they both give him a congratulatory hug. "You're going to be something special, Jarvis; keep up the good work," Michael says as he pats Jarvis on his back. Michael then shifts his attention to Dan. "Not too bad for an old man; good job, dad!" Dan smiles at Michael and Sarah. "We appreciate all the praise, but with all due respect, we have work to do." They both nod and head towards their personal vehicles while waving bye to the boys and Dan. Sarah and Michael both have shifts to work at their jobs. Dan has always required his children to maintain summer jobs while living in his house. Since teenagers, they have always done so and never complained about it.

Sunday creates a sense of leisure, as Dan and the boys enjoy their time executing the passing drills. Dan calls the boys over to help him set the cones up in a new formation to take the training up a notch. While the boys are assisting Dan with the cones, they hear blaring rap music coming from a car on the street passing by Dan's house. The boys both stop and become distracted, because it is rare to hear that type of music in a neighborhood like the one Dan resides in. And this is also the type of music they like. The boys peek over the shrubs in Dan's yard and see a gray sedan moving slowly past the property. They cannot see who is in the car but whoever is driving makes a turn on an adjacent street and drives back towards Dan's house. Dan is not paying attention to the noise and continues moving the cones in various patterns throughout the massive yard. The boys decide to head towards the side of the house to get a better look. As they become visible to the driver from the side of Dan's yard, the car stops directly beside the boys. The music volume lowers as a head peeks through the passenger side of a brand new 1987 Nissan Maxima. The boys instantly recognize the driver as 1984 Virginia High-School Player of the Year and Heritage Park Phenom, Mitchell Baptiste Jr. He is named after his deceased Haitian father, but everyone calls him Macho. Macho and his mother moved to Virginia from New Jersey to be closer to her family after his father was murdered by drug dealers. He, like Jarvis and Corey, got singled out by Dan and stayed at the Butler house just four short years ago. Macho is now twenty and going into his junior year at the biggest university in the state. He is the star running back and slated for the NFL draft after graduation. Macho is beyond handsome with smooth dark brown skin, perfect, straight white teeth, and shiny black hair with a swirl of circular waves called 360s. He is not tall, maybe five feet, nine inches, but his stocky muscular build makes him a force on the field. Most yards per carry in the conference two years in a row. Macho was also named the NCAA Rookie of the Year in 1985. Macho is a big deal in Division 1 college football, and the boys cannot believe he is in Dan's neighborhood.

Macho motions for the boys to come over from the passenger window. They ran over to the side of Macho's car and could not contain themselves. "Yo Macho, I'm Corey, and this is Jarvis; he's about to be the star QB for Heritage High." "What up little dudes? Y'all practicing with Coach Dan?" Macho daps up both boys while questioning them. Corey responds, "Yup, trying to get like you." Jarvis asks, "What are you doing around here, Macho?" Macho responds, "I stayed here and practiced with Dan a few years ago, just like y'all." Corey looks dead into Macho's eyes, and they start an intense conversation without saying a word. Corey breaks the silence, "Oh yeah, so you stayed here too, huh?" Macho nods and asks, "How y'all holding up in all this heat?" Corey is reading between the lines and responds accordingly, "We doing as good as expected; the heat is unbearable at times." Corey never breaks eye contact with Macho. Jarvis is confused by the bizarre interaction between Macho and Corey but plays it cool and lets his friend control the conversation. Macho continues, "I really just stopped when I saw y'all out here practicing. I wanted to make sure everything was okay." Jarvis is perplexed by all the nurturing questions. Why is Macho so concerned about them? Corey responds, "We okay for now, I guess." But his eyes are locked with Macho's as if to say, "We're not safe." Macho catches the look in Corey's eyes, and there is an implicit understanding that the boys are in the same danger that he was in while staying at the Butler home years before. The bizarre silence is broken once Dan realizes that the boys are on the street talking to a familiar face. Dan yells, "Hey Macho, how are you buddy?" Dan is standing in the yard and waving both arms like an idiot. Macho just nods his chin upwards, cordially acknowledging Dan's salutation without verbally responding to his question. Dan is visibly nervous and unsure whether to interrupt Macho's interaction with the boys. Dan does not want Macho to become too chummy with Jarvis, and especially Corey, as his secret could become exposed. Dan decides that he must preserve his lifestyle at any cost, so he hesitantly walks in the direction of Macho's car. Just before Dan is about to step off the curb, Mary calls out, "Dan, come get the phone; it's Rick. He says that it's important." Dan stops in his tracks. Macho, Corey, and Jarvis all turn and stare at him. He is torn between ignoring Mary and continuing towards the car or turning to get the phone call. Dan is frozen and indecisive. Mary calls out again, "Dan, come get this call now please. Rick really needs to speak with you." Dan reluctantly turns and hastily heads towards the patio where Mary is holding the corded phone from the kitchen. Corey and Jarvis turn their attention back to Macho. Macho quickly reaches for a bookbag laying in his passenger seat, riffles past some cologne and a hairbrush to retrieve a pen and notebook. He rips off a small corner from one of the pages and writes down his number. "Take this and call me if you need to umm, PRACTICE." Macho locks eyes with Corey again with the understanding this is not about practice. He passes the piece of paper out of the window. Jarvis goes to grab it, but Corey snatches it instead, and says, "Thanks Macho. I'll keep this safe, and we will definitely be calling you soon." Macho follows up with instructions, "I'm pretty busy, but you can call that number anytime and leave a message with my mom; she usually knows how to find me." Corey folds the paper into a small ball and places it in the bottom of his shoe. Jarvis finds all of this to be rather odd but decides he will question Corey about it later. Just as Corey gets his shoe back on, Dan runs out of the sliding door towards Macho's car. Macho sees Dan heading his way immediately says, "Well, I'm late for something; you guys take care, and don't forget to call me for training." Macho daps Corey and Jarvis before pulling off. Corey silently mouths to him "Thank you." Macho nods and screeches down the street, music blaring again. Dan runs into the street. "Geez, why did he leave so suddenly? Did I do something? What did he say?" Dan seems desperate for answers as he badgers the boys. "What did Macho say? What did you talk about?" Corey responds to Dan calmly, "Nothing. He just offered to help us train; that's it. He didn't even mention you." Dan looks at Corey and catches on to his condescending tone. "Jarvis, get ready to do some passing routes with me. Corey, two miles since you want to have such a smart mouth," Dan says while standing eye to eye with Corey. Corey doesn't even flinch; he puffs up his chest, gives Dan a contemptuous smirk, and starts running before Dan can even start his stopwatch or blow his whistle. Corey's smug attitude is becoming a concern for Dan, and he is unsure of how to handle it. Dan and Jarvis walk towards the yard to continue practice. Dan is becoming frustrated and needs to come up with a new plan to humble and subdue Corey. For now, he must put less focus on his lust for Jarvis and more on his athletic abilities. FOR NOW!

CHAPTER 9

"PLAN UNRAVELS"

A lmost three weeks have now flown by, and Dan is no closer to executing his plan than he was when the boys first arrived. Time is slipping away, and Dan realizes that he will not be able to nurture the relationship between him and Jarvis like he hoped. He is frustrated both sexually and mentally. The only positive takeaway is that the boys have developed into tremendously solid football players in a very short time frame. Even Corey is showing signs of becoming an integral part of the team, beyond water boy, as Dan previously planned. But none of this is enough for Dan, and he is feeling immense pressure to ditch his calm, collected demeanor for one that more closely resembles that of his father. "Take what I want and worry about the fall out later" runs through Dan's veins. He feels as though he deserves Jarvis at this point. He has spent so much time and money on both boys. Dan feels that he is in the beginning stages of insanity. He always gets his way, and this situation is causing Dan a great deal of anxiety. He has even started excessively biting his nails, a habit he had as a child growing up in a dysfunctional home with, "the Tyrant." The hard reality for Dan is that the 4th of July is this coming weekend, and that will mark just one more week before the boys leave. Dan is in panic mode and decides to escalate his plans. He may even need to carry some of his deviancies beyond his summer training, something he rarely does due to the amount of risk should someone see them. But this thing has been carried out too long, and Dan is definitely going to have his way, even if someone has to get hurt.

It is Thursday night, and the boys are up watching sitcoms with Sarah, Michael, and Mary. Jarvis and Corey are almost like family now. Most of the Butlers seem to be comfortable and pleased with their presence. Dan, still operating as a recluse, is off in his study and not being a part of anything his family does. Around 10:00 p.m., Dan has had enough of the laughing and chatter going on in the living room. If he can't enjoy himself, no one can. He suddenly hops off the couch in his study, marches into the living room, and orders everyone to go to their own room. He turns the TV off and stands in front of it with his arms folded. Everyone sits puzzled for a minute, thinking maybe Dan is joking. After they realize he is not moving or smiling, they start to slowly get up and go off to their bedrooms. Sarah gives Dan the coldest stare as she shuffles past him towards her room. He doesn't even acknowledge her confrontational stance, his eyes fixed on Corey. Deep down inside, Dan blames Corey for his inability to get close to Jarvis. Numerous foiled opportunities with Corey at the center of all the seemingly coincidental antics is making Dan resent ever bringing him along with Jarvis. Dan's deteriorating mental state is to the point that he wants to harm Corey physically. But how could he ever explain Corey getting hurt while in his home? All these thoughts are running through Dan's head as he watches the boys solemnly drag themselves off to their room. Mary just sits alone on the sofa as the once boisterous living room is now quiet and empty, except for her and Dan. Mary hasn't moved a muscle since Dan made everyone go to bed. He turns and asks Mary, "Are you coming to bed?" She doesn't respond, just appears dejected, looking at the TV as if it is still on. Dan suddenly realizes he may have overreacted in his moment of despair but remains unapologetic as turns to go to bed without further acknowledging Mary. What's done is done, and he cannot take it back, but he will find a way to make it up tomorrow. Afterall, everyone can be bought, and that's just what Dan plans to do. Dan cuts the lights off in the living room, leaving Mary in the dark, his final insensitive act of the evening. Dan doesn't care; he will fix it in the morning.

It's Friday morning, one day until the 4th of July, and all in the Butler household are up decorating and prepping for the holiday. Even Dan is up assisting Michael with the heavier workload. The boys are enjoying craft type details with Mary and Sarah. It is as if they picked up from the night before. There is so much laughter and enjoyment coming from their section of the patio. Dan controls his anger this time, though seeing them all so happy annoys him. No one has really spoken to Dan all morning except Michael, who doesn't ever seem phased by his father's behavior. It is nearing lunch time, and Dan decides to interrupt their activities with an indirect apology for his boorish outburst from Thursday night. Dan clears his throat to get everyone's attention, this time, with an announcement he thinks everyone will enjoy. "Alright everyone, let's take a little break from all the work; we're going to head out and grab lunch at Felder's (a popular local cafeteria style restaurant). Then me and the boys will head over to the sporting goods store to get a few things for the season. How does that sound?" All seems forgotten as the kids and the boys almost immediately drop what they are doing and appear excited by Dan's announcement. All except Mary. Her disenchanted reaction does not go unnoticed by Dan. He actually expects this type of reaction from Mary and plans accordingly. He quietly places an envelope full of money in her lap, kisses her forehead, and tells her to go shopping with the kids after lunch. With no change in her somber facial expression, she takes the envelope, stuffs it in her purse, and quickly strides towards the door. "Come on kids. You too boys. Dan, we'll meet at Felder's." Dan is shocked that Mary has instructed everyone to leave without him but shrugs and gets into his own car to meet everyone at the restaurant.

By now, the entire family is completely full and lethargic from the big meal they have just eaten. Dan and Mary both had a very conservative helping compared to his kids and the boys. Felder's is well known for their burgers, which is what everyone at the table ate. The restaurant has steady traffic for late lunch on a Friday afternoon. Everyone recognizes Dan and cordially addresses him during the outing. The whole community knows that he has recruits at his house over the summer, and they are almost always black. Which is why no one questions a family of white people with two Black boys. In 1987, this would surely have caused a scene if not for Dan's standing in the community and the understanding that he is training these boys for the upcoming football season. The boys are leaning in their chairs with their bellies protruding. Jarvis had to unbutton his jean shorts to keep from cutting off his circulation. Dan sneakily caught a peek out of the corner of his eye. Corey had on an old pair of sweatpants that were a size too small. Needless to say, Corey is looking forward to the trip to the sporting goods store. But Dan has no intention of spending a dime on Corey. As a matter of fact, he wants to attempt to separate Jarvis from Corey for at least a couple of minutes so that he can confront him about his behavior. Just one of the thoughts swirling through Dan's mind as he lets his meal digest. Mary abruptly interrupts everyone's silent intermission by asking Sarah and Michael to take the boys over to the toy claw-crane machines up front for a bit. She pulls ten dollars from her purse and softly says, "This should hold you for a while." She hands the money to Sarah. Both boys' eyes get big, and Corey hops up and rushes over to the machines, Sarah, and Michael in tow. Jarvis is slow to get up but makes sure he thanks Mary and Dan before he joins Sarah, Michael, and Corey. Mary smiles at him warmly and then turns to Dan, who missed everything that has just happened, as he seems to be in his own world. "Dan, can we talk? I wanted to run something by you." Dan stares at Mary as if he has just woken up from a deep sleep. "Sure, what's wrong now?" Mary ignores Dan's cold response. She launches into a full rant, mostly about how she would like to take a more active role in Jarvis' and Corey's life moving forward. She rambles on and on for what seems to be an eternity for Dan, but in reality, it is only about three minutes. Dan sits quietly while Mary petitions about wanting to do more productive things with her time now that their kids are adults and will be living their own lives soon. She feels that she has made a connection with the boys and wants to continue to nurture their bond. She also mentions wanting to mentor and volunteer at the high school where Dan works and that she would appreciate him putting in a word for her. Dan listens intently while Mary gabs, even nodding on occasion as if he is empathic to her plight. Mary finally takes a breath as a tear rolls down her cheek. Dan waits for a second, then cautiously asks, "Are you finished?" Mary looks down into her lap and nods "yes." Dan places his index finger under her chin to gently lift her face and make intense eye contact with her. As he gazes into her eyes, she feels so connected to Dan in that moment. He warmly caresses her face, leans in close, almost as if he is going to kiss her. Mary closes her eyes and parts her lips in anticipation. Dan bypasses the opportunity and whispers in her ear, "NO." All in the same motion, he stands, drops a twenty-dollar bill on the table and briskly strides toward the restaurant entrance. He stops only for a second to motion to the boys it's time to go. Mary, still sitting, is devastated by what Dan just did. She desperately wants to break down crying, but in true Butler fashion, she holds it together publicly. Mary wipes her eyes with a handkerchief she has in her purse. She stands up, proudly tilts her chin high, and gracefully strolls to the front of the restaurant where Sarah and Micheal are waiting, as if nothing happened.

Dan holds the door to Levitz Sporting Goods as the boys excitedly file in and immediately run over to the shoe section. Though Levitz is local, and family owned, they are known for carrying an impressive inventory of all the popular brands of the time. Adidas, Nike, Reebok. The boys can hardly keep their composure around so many options. One of the clerks recognizes Dan. A tall, slender built man, mid-twenties, short blond buzz cut nods as Dan and the boys walk into the store. There aren't many patrons looking for sporting goods on this day, and Dan is thankful for that. Jarvis is in heaven as he scans every row of displayed sneakers. Corey seems more interested in the clothing section and browses through a display table full of shorts. Dan briefly scans the entire store, then he swiftly grabs Corey by the collar and drags him into the dressing room without anyone seeming to pay attention. Dan releases him and tells him to shut up. Corey, with tears running from his eyes, starts pleading with Dan not to hurt him. Dan presses his forearm against Corey's throat with all his strength. "I don't know what your problem is, but I am tired of your bullshit. You keep disrespecting me, and I am going to put an end to it now! Your ass is going home after the fourth. I spoke to your mom, and I am sending you back Sunday. Now what do you have to say about that?" Dan hadn't spoken to Corey's mom, nor did he intend on sending him home; he just hoped to scare him enough to stop with the extreme behavior. Corey's entire body is trembling as he starts to relive his past trauma. Dan ignores Corey's spasms and continues to threaten him. "I could kill your ass right now with my bare hands, but if I hear a peep out of you before Sunday, I just may gut you with my hunting knife!" Just in that moment, Corey's body goes completely limp. Dan catches him before he hits the floor. Dan is in shock and not sure what to do with Corey, as he is afraid that he just killed him. Just as Dan is about to run into the storefront and get the clerk to call an ambulance, Corey opens his eyes. He appears disoriented but manages to shake off what was probably a panic attack. Dan takes a deep sigh of relief while Corey gathers himself. But Dan's excitement about dodging a potential murder charge is dashed when he realizes that Corey has urinated in his sweatpants. Dan's emotions escalate to an extreme, understanding that not only has Corey once again caused a spectacle but he will also need to buy new clothes for him to wear outside of the store. Dan smacks Corey in the face out of frustration and tells him to stay there. Dan quickly strides out of the dressing room, straight over to the shorts that Corey had previously been looking at before Dan grabbed him. He intently shuffles through the pile and picks out a pair he thinks should fit Corey and pulls the price tag off. Dan then storms back to the dressing room, throws the shorts at Corey who is now in a fetal position on the dressing room floor. He is still crying and trembling as Dan firmly whispers, "Get your shit together. NOW! Take those nasty pants off and throw them in the garbage when you're done." Dan is about to leave the dressing room area, but he stops and turns to give Corey one more blow. He cracks the door so that nothing, but the center of his face is seen by Corey. "You are so pathetic. I don't know why someone like Jarvis would ever hang around a loser like you." Dan then slams the door and strides back into the storefront and over the register. Dan hands the tag to the clerk and tells him that he is paying for the shorts that the young man in the dressing room will be wearing. While Dan is waiting to pay for the shorts, he glances over to see Jarvis, who he had almost forgotten about with all the commotion. Jarvis is still browsing the sneaker selection and again, in true Jarvis oblivion, he doesn't notice that Dan and Corey have been gone for at least five minutes. Dan feels a sense of calm when he sees Jarvis' face and informs the clerk that he will be adding some more items to his tab. The clerk nods okay as Dan walks over to join Jarvis. Dan stands directly behind Jarvis, who had not noticed he is there. "See anything you like?" Jarvis is startled by Dan's presence. "Coach, oh my God; you scared me. I didn't know you were here." Jarvis clutches his chest to catch his breath. Both Dan and Jarvis chuckle as he regains his composure. "Yeah, I kinda like these ones Coach. Do you like 'em?" Jarvis holds up a pair of popular high-top basketball shoes. Dan responds, "I like them if you do. Let's get them, my treat." Jarvis smiles as he replies, "Thanks Coach. I appreciate it." Jarvis' excitement is fleeting, as he suddenly notices that Corey is nowhere in sight. Jarvis begins to intensively audit the store for any sign of his best friend. "Hey Coach, where is Corey? I haven't seen him since we walked in." Dan is slightly annoyed that Jarvis is worried about Corey at this moment. "The last time I saw him, he was in the dressing room trying on some clothes. I guess he will be out in a minute." To Dan's dismay, Jarvis starts to walk towards the dressing room. Dan is just about to make up diversion, so Jarvis won't walk into the dressing area and see his friend in the condition in which he was left. Just as Jarvis is about to enter the dressing room area, Corey walks out as if nothing happened. Dan is dumbfounded at Corey's transformation from the mess he last saw lying on the floor sobbing to what he is currently seeing. Dan cannot figure out why Corey appears so neat. Then it dawns on him. Corey must've covertly picked out a shirt in addition to the shorts and now has on an entirely new outfit. Jarvis is excited to see his friend look so distinguished. The two buddies exchange some high fives and laugh as they walk back over to Dan. Corey stands directly in front of Dan and looks him in both eyes and hands him the price tag from the shirt. Feeling as though he has nothing to lose, Corey is back to his mischievous behavior. Dan had seen a side of him that he would never be able to explain or live down. His only goal now is to protect Jarvis. Corey feels that his life is worthless after everything he had just experienced, but Jarvis is worth saving. With a renewed sense of purpose, Corey promises himself to be brave from this point forward until he is sure that his friend is out of harm's way.

There is an awkward silence the entire ride home from the sporting goods store. Dan, Jarvis, and Corey all sit in the front of the car without hardly saying a word. Jarvis is aware something is amidst between Corey and Dan, but he is unsure what to make of it, so he just keeps quiet. All that Jarvis can surmise is that, even in silence, Dan seems about as mad as he has ever seen him. Dan did end up buying each boy more clothes and shoes than expected, but this can't be why he is seething the entire ride home. All the veins in Dan's forearm are protruding as he grips the steering wheel with extreme force, driving a lot faster than usual and occasionally mumbling to himself. Jarvis is sitting in the middle of Dan and Corey and acts as a buffer between the two on the bench seat. Corey gazes out of the window and doesn't even appear to blink, his blank stare pierces the passenger glass. Jarvis has never seen Corey like this and instantly becomes nervous that Dan may have told him the secret about his mom. Dan is livid thinking about how dumb he is for allowing Corey into his home and how he has ruined his plans for Jarvis. Dan feels himself unraveling at a rapid rate and has uncontrollable feelings of emotion he hasn't experienced since he was a teen. He wants to inflict pain on Corey for all the drama he has caused. He almost wishes he'd ended up in the hospital or worse, after that fiasco at the store. Dan notices out of the corner of his eye that Corey is in a trance-like state and is fearful of retaliation after the day's events. Dan was not serious about sending Corey home Sunday like he had threatened earlier, but he is now thinking that it isn't such a bad idea. He would need to think of a reason for doing such, but he had until Sunday morning to come up with something that made sense. The whole ordeal has Dan exhausted, and he is just ready for the day to be over so that he can rest. The surroundings start to look familiar to the boys as Dan gets closer to home. They finally arrive at the rear of the house after what seems like the longest car ride ever. Dan screeches into the driveway under the carport, and without saying a word, exits the car, slams the door, and heads towards the patio. The boys are still seated. Jarvis is alarmed by what he has just witnessed. "What's eating him and are you okay man? What's up with you?" asks Jarvis, trying to gauge the situation and see if Corey's strange behavior is in any way related to his intimacies with Jackie. Corey finally peels his eyes away from the passenger window he had been intensely staring out of the entire way home. Now facing Jarvis, he says, "I'm good Jay; let's go in and enjoy our new shit and eat like kings on this honkey's dime." They both laugh and grab the bags full of items Dan purchased for them. Jarvis feels a sense of relief, as it seems Corey is still not aware of his secret. They walk slowly towards the patio with so many unanswered questions between them. Jarvis wonders what the beef between Corey and Dan is, and if his secret is still safe or if Corey is pretending not to know. Corey is ashamed of his past and feels humiliated by Dan after what took place at the store earlier. Corey is also scared that Dan will be sending him back home, leaving a green, naive Jarvis to defend himself against a pervert. In this single moment of calm, just before they get to the steps of the patio entrance to the house, Corey throws his right arm around Jarvis' neck. "I got your back forever, Jay. I hope you know that. My best friend since Claremont Garden Apartments; we all we got!" Jarvis smiles at his best friend and returns the gesture. They walk into the Butler home, arms around each other's necks, closer than they have ever been in their lives. Brothers, only separated by blood. They inaudibly vow allegiance to one another, two Black boys surviving in a world that is uninviting to them. But, in the interim, there's always the 4th of July!

It's getting late, and the boys are excited about the festivities planned for tomorrow. They are about to get ready for bed but are up playing with the game console Dan purchased for them. The volume is down low, so they do not disturb anyone else in the house. They haven't seen Dan since they returned but assume he is in his office next to them, where he usually is. Corey is nervous but needs to have an important conversation with Jarvis. As the glare from the TV shines on their faces, Corey whispers to Jarvis, "What do you think of

Dan?" Jarvis is confused by the question. "What do you mean? I guess he's okay.. Why are you asking?" Corey pauses the game then asks again, "Like what do you really think of Coach Dan? Why do you think we're here? Why do you think my ass is here? I can't play no damn football; anybody with two eyes can see that shit," Corey quiets back down to a whisper once he senses himself becoming too animated and raising his voice. "Look Jarvis, just take my word please. I think we're in danger here, and if you're too green to see what's going on, then just trust me. We need to get out of here. Tonight, if you're ready." Jarvis is astonished at what Corey is suggesting. "Dude, are you crazy? You're really bugging right now. I think we're both here because the coach saw something special in us and wants to help us become amazing football players so that we can go to college and get away from these small towns and cities. Wait, that's not what you think?" Corey laughs at Jarvis' impression of Dan and his inability to process what is truly going on. Corey decides at that moment not to disclose Dan's full intent for him; he does not think Jarvis will understand or even believe him. Jarvis begins to go on and on and about how good this family has been to them, and that Dan is a good man and only wants the best for them. Corey listens about as long as he possibly can before stopping Jarvis mid-sentence. "Look, I get it, Jay. Dan is this and that to you, blah blah blah, but do you trust me when I tell you as your best friend, your brother, WE ARE IN DANGER? We need to leave here ASAP!" Jarvis lets out a long sigh and placed both hands on his face. Conflicted by loyalty to his friend but also the uncertainty of his future as a football player, high-school student, and beyond. He is also scared of how his mother and father will react to him just leaving Dan's home abruptly without a real explanation to offer why. If they go through with this, they will surely not be a part of the team this season, or possibly ever. How would they explain their choice to leave? Corey chimes in before Jarvis can respond, "Look, without me saying too much, I honestly think you're in greater danger than me. I know you can't see it, but you're not safe here Jay." Jarvis finally looks up and says, "Okay, I trust you, and I am willing to do this. But first, we need to have a plan, and secondly, can we do this tomorrow night? I think my mom is out of town, and I want some food from the grill. I also want to see the fireworks Sarah and Michael showed us earlier. Can we at least do that man?" Corey looks his friend in the face and nods "yes." Corey quickly responds, "Who told you I don't have a plan nigga? I got this! Remember when I was staring out of the car window earlier, looking like a psycho. I was memorizing the route so that we can safely get to the nearest payphone and call Macho to come get us." Corey smiles and winks. "Hopefully, we can stay at Macho's house until morning, then we call our parents and tell them we were just ready to come home early. We will just have to deal with the consequences later." Corey seems to have thought this all out thoroughly, which impresses Jarvis. The time they have spent at Dan's house has shown Jarvis a side of Corey he has never seen before. Courage and determination, two words that he thought he would never be able to associate with his friend. Jarvis suddenly becomes sad. "What about all our things? Our clothes, our shoes, and even this video game? Are we just going to leave all this stuff behind?" Corey replies optimistically, "We leave at midnight. Maybe 1:00 a.m., pack light, only what you can fit in your backpack; they're just things. Take only what you need for now, and maybe we can get Sarah or Michael to bring our things later. They honestly love us you know; I think they would help us if need be. Plus, I think Sarah has a crush on me; she will do what I say." Jarvis gives Corey a blank stare in response to the last part of his statement, then they both laugh a bit at the thought of Sarah actually liking anything about Corey. "You're crazy if you think that girl wants either of us." But Jarvis does agree with the idea that Michael, Sarah, and Mrs. Butler have their best interest in mind. "Okay, so tomorrow it is." They shake hands then a tight embrace. "Love you Jay," says an emotional Corey, realizing tomorrow could change their whole lives. "Stop being a fag," Jarvis says jokingly in an effort to lighten the mood. "I'm kidding. Let's get ready for bed; we got a big day tomorrow!" Corey cuts the game off, and both boys lay down for the night.

CHAPTER 10

"NOW OR NEVER"

Everyone is up early and excited about the 4th of July. There is a yearly parade that takes place in the center of town on Main Street every year. Just about everyone in the community usually attends. This will be both Jarvis' and Corey's first year in attendance, and they can hardly wait. The parade is usually followed up by a cookout at the Butler home. There is usually a large turnout of past players, their family members, and many of the neighbors. They all make it a point to show up every year for the Butler 4th of July celebration. But the Butler's have opted to have a smaller gathering this year, as Dan expressed that he simply does not feel up to it. The preparation is exhausting, and everyone seems pleased with having a lighter workload. They are still planning to have a crowd of twenty or so. Just a few neighbors this year. Sarah and Michael have also invited a few of their close friends. The boys are up helping Michael with some finishing touches to the exterior decorations. Both boys look amazing as they adorn the new clothes Dan purchased them the day before. They both are badly in need of haircuts, as they have not been able to get to a barber shop while staying with the Butlers, especially Corey. Michael once offered to take them to his barber. Both boys flat out refused, afraid to let a white man cut their hair for fear he would not do a good job. But Jarvis and Corey manage to brush, comb, and groom their locks to a presentable state. Mary seems beyond pleased at their appearance and has taken multiple opportunities to comment on how handsome are. Mary has her camera out and takes tons of pictures of Michael, Sarah, and the boys. "I just can't get over how handsome you both look. I am so proud of you both." Corey is especially moved by Mary's kind words because no one in his life ever says these types of things to him. He doesn't even know how to react to the barrage of compliments from Mary. Dan just rolls his eyes in disgust and reminds himself that Corey will be gone by this time tomorrow, and everything will be perfect. Dan hasn't yet informed the family of his plan to send Corey home. He does not want to interrupt everyone's excitement for the holiday, so he will let them know his plan in the morning. He will tell them that Corey's mother has a vacation planned, and he is traveling with his family out of town. Then, he will tell Corey's mother that Corey is acting out, because he wants to go home. Dan knows that Jackie will believe him over her own son. He also feels that Jackie and Milton will deal with Corey harshly for misbehaving at the Butler home and squandering his opportunity to play football. Dan literally smiles at the thought of Corey being punished. He put a lot of thought into this plan, and Dan is certain it will all work out perfectly.

The parade is a hit! Jarvis and Corey have just about exhausted themselves with all the excitement. They are both intoxicated with delight. Corey and Jarvis got the opportunity to meet so many kids their age, and Dan introduced them to everyone as his upcoming prodigies. The boys were treated like superstars, and they were well received by everyone in the Heritage Park. Jarvis and Corey felt like celebrities, and they cherished every moment of the community gushing over them. Dan, Mary, the kids, and the boys excused themselves from the parade a bit early so that they could put the finishing touches on the barbeque they have underway for their guests. They arrive back at the Butler home and immediately get to work with Dan barking instructions in every direction. Dan prides himself on his skills managing the grill and has Mary bring all the meat out for him to start cooking. There are sausage links, hot dogs, fresh ground beef hamburger patties, barbeque chicken (Sarah does not eat red meat), and a few New York strips. The steaks are not for the guests, just the Butler residents to eat later. There is also corn on the cob, potato salad, baked beans, and freshly tossed salad, all prepared by Mary. The boys, as usual, are excited about the spread and are trying to hurry and complete the tasks Dan has assigned so that they can watch him prepare the meat on the grill. Everyone seems to be in a good mood today, even Mary and Dan. They are all helping one another, and overall, are cheerful and jubilant. Dan knows that he is getting rid of Corey, and he can now spend some much-needed quality time with Jarvis; he can hardly wait! But Corey is also excited that he will be killing Dan's dreams of doing to Jarvis what was done to him. Jarvis is just as excited about the food at this point. Mary has just quietly decided to go through with her plan of helping the boys and other youth, as she discussed with Dan at the restaurant, despite his objection. Her spirit has been broken so many times throughout her marriage to Dan, but for the first time in all their years together, Mary has blatantly chosen to defy his decision on a matter. She is afraid on the inside of how he will react, but Mary has made her mind up. She wants to be more than just Dan Butler's wife. She feels as though God has given her a bigger mission, and it involves helping young people in the community. Mary gently smiles to herself and is pleased with her choice. Everyone in the Butler home is diligently getting set up for the company they had coming over. The festivities are to begin at 5:00 p.m. It is about 3:00 p.m., and they are well on pace to be ready for their guests.

The celebration is under way, and the entire Butler estate is buzzing with excitement and activity. A few unexpected people show up, but the Butlers welcome them with open arms. Rick shows up this year, and he has brought a date. A short, stocky, brown-skinned woman with very long black hair named Toni. She is delightful, vivacious, and full of conversation. Not the type anyone would expect to be interested in a guy like Rick. Undoubtedly the first time anyone had ever seen Rick with a woman. All who know him are overly concerned about his personal life, though no one ever spoke about it. This would put a very nosy and judgmental community with traditional family values at ease. Of course, the news of Rick showing up to Dan's house with a woman would be all over Heritage Park before nightfall. Most of the people in attendance had met Jarvis and Corey earlier that day at the parade and are already familiar with them. But, only at the barbeque did everyone get to meet the boys' appetite. They ate nonstop during the entire gathering. Corey is actually a bit more reserved than normal but munching, nonetheless. Everyone appears to be having a blast; there isn't a face that is not smiling among the guests. There are so many side conversations taking place between all the unlikely personalities. Dan really gets into the moment and decides to bring out some aged bourbon that he had received as a gift many years ago. Dan doesn't usually drink, but caught up in the moment, he convinces himself that a couple of sips would not hurt. Mary, the boys, and Sarah are the only ones not savoring the alcohol Dan provides for everyone. Michael is not allowed to drink too much, but Dan did allow him to have a cup of what he affectionately called "the golden honey." A term "the Tyrant" favored in his many moments of extreme intoxication. The more the bottle is passed, the more everyone's speech slurs, the laughter gets louder, and conversations seem more inappropriate. Corey and Jarvis just watch as all the adults, with every gulp, lose control of their rationale. Corey is accustomed to these chaotic drunken episodes in his own home and is not affected by their behavior. But he does observe something that he find odd. Rick is acting like everyone else, impaired, but is hardly drinking at all. He is basically taking small sips from his initial cup full. Corey is intrigued by this and wondered why he is behaving in such an odd manner. Jarvis, not really paying attention of course, is just sitting back on one of the patio cushions enjoying the beautiful sunset that's beginning to take place. Dan, who is usually very reserved, is suddenly the life of the party. No one had ever seen him so boisterous and animated. Most of the guests welcomed Dan's less frigid demeanor and mirrored his affable temperament, while Mary and Sarah sat in the rear of the patio, glaring in disgust. This behavior went on for more than an hour, only getting more rowdy by the minute. Amid all the excitement, Dan hops up and says, "Do y'all want to see something cool?" The guests react by cheering, clearly indicating "yes!" He runs into the house and immediately returns with a small, wooden box. Dan sits back down in his seat and sets the box on the table in front of him. The crowd gets quiet, not knowing what to expect inside. Dan opens the beautifully engraved top slowly. Everyone moves in close to get a better look. Then alas, Dan carefully removes a WWII German Luger Pistol. It had a long black shiny barrel and a wooden handle that adorned a neatly engraved broken cross Nazi symbol. It was exquisite and in immaculate condition. Dan briefly explains how he retrieved the gun from his dad's house when he was placed in the nursing home. Dan said that his father would often ask where his gun was and request that it be brought to him, but Dan knew that he could not have a gun in the facility that he stayed in. Dan goes on and on of how his father told him that the gun belonged to one of Hitler's top lieutenants. Rick interrupts Dan's story, as he could sense that the crowd is losing interest. He asks Dan if he'd ever shot it before. Dan replies that he had not but maybe tonight he would test it out. Dan and Corey lock eyes in an instant following that statement. A concerned Mary overhears this as well and swiftly grabs the gun and the box and heads back inside. Fireworks are going off in the background nonstop by neighbors of the Butler home.

Indecorous and shameless is the scene on the patio. Sarah and Michael decide to take charge of the situation by bringing out the fireworks they had planned to display for that evening. The Butler children call Jarvis and Corey over to assist them with the set up as they head to the rear of the yard, away from the patio partygoers. The boys zealously follow them, eager to view the illuminations to come. No one on the patio seems to notice the kids heading away from the patio except Rick. Even in the frenzy surrounding him, he seems to keep a watchful eye on all activities stirring. Just as Rick is observing his surroundings, Corey is observing Rick. Corey is increasingly becoming weary of Rick's odd behavior on this night. He is acutely aware of how close Dan and Rick are and begins to wonder if Rick has the same perversions for young boys as Dan. This all solidifies to Corey that he and Jarvis must escape the Butler home tonight. The fact that everyone has been drinking and probably not paying attention plays into their favor. By now, Dan has started yelling profane obscenities and telling lewd jokes to the dismay of all attendees, but mostly, Dan's wife. Mary is absolutely appalled and humiliated by Dan's extreme behavior. Her heart is telling her to watch over him and make sure he doesn't further embarrass himself, but her mind is telling her that he is an adult and sealing his own fate. Mary ultimately decides to go to bed and worry about cleaning up the mess and checking on Dan and the kids in the morning. Sarah waves the boys back for safety as she and Michael light the first set of fireworks without any warning to the patio guests. BANG! The sound must've startled everyone within a half mile radius. The luminance display lights up the black sky with a beautiful burst of brilliance. The shocked guests all halt their shenanigans in awe of the explosive glow overhead. Corey and Jarvis cheer with delight as the brilliant white sparkles cascade over the Butler home and all of Beaumont Estates. For the first time in hours, the party goers are silenced, enthralled at the sight of the lights. Sarah had achieved two goals at once. Firstly, she was able to get the patio party participants to calm down. Secondly, she wanted to do something exciting for Jarvis and Corey. Sarah stood in the shadows, arms crossed with a facetious grin on her face as Michael continued to light fireworks, one after another. Mission accomplished! Jarvis is cheering uncontrollably, and by the time Michael had set off the tenth round of rockets, so were the patio participants. Corey sat back, leaning on one of Dan's cars under the carport. He just scans the yard in slow motion. Emotions are starting to catch up to him. He just intimately took in all the sights at that moment, everyone seemingly enjoying the occasion in their own way. Corey wondered what life would be like in the next twenty-four hours. He decides to hold on to this visual scene for the rest of his life. He had experienced so much despair in his young life; it is beautiful to see everyone in his presence experiencing the height of exhilaration. A tear ran down his face, not out of sorrow or pity, but with a sudden feeling of optimism for the future. For the first time in his life, Corey feels as if he no longer wants to take what life is giving him and now can vividly see himself creating his own happiness. With everything that had transpired in the last week, Corey had forgotten that his birthday is tomorrow, July 5th. In just a couple of short hours, he will be fifteen years old. 'WOW,' he thought Corey as he realizes that his tumultuous youth had been riddled with so much adversity, he had never even had a real birthday party. No one had ever celebrated him, not like the people in this yard at this very moment. This alone is enough to inspire him. He will be heading into the tenth grade at one of the top-rated high schools in the state. So, what if his home life is difficult? There's only three more years to go. Surely, he could persevere until then. He has made it this far; he isn't about to quit now. There is too much to live for. Maybe Sarah, Michael, and Mrs. Butler would help him along the way. Maybe he could join the military after graduation. Or maybe he and Jarvis would attend college together. Perhaps he could get a good job like Jarvis' father. Corey feels a surge of anticipation for the possibilities of what the future holds for him. He could look forward to things like having a girlfriend, getting a job, or even driving a car. Corey smiles so big with the realization that no matter what, it would all be alright. The worst part is behind him. He would no longer allow his past nor his volatile home life to define him. As soon as he and Jarvis could get away from Dan, it would start a new chapter for him.

CHAPTER 11

(CONCLUSION) "UNLIKELY HEROES"

Corey sits quietly on the floor, eyes as wide as silver dollars, gazing at the digital clock on the nightstand, "1:26" it reads. It seems like time is dragging on with each minute. Even though Corey feels confident everyone has left for the night and the Butler family is now sound asleep, he waits so that Jarvis can get a bit of extra rest. They have a long night ahead of them, and Corey wants to make sure that Jarvis would be sharp and focused. He has all the belongings that he wants to carry in a small nap sack tucked neatly under the bed that Jarvis is laying on. He's taking all the clothes that Dan purchased and will leave most of his old stuff here. He is sure most of it would be tossed once the dust settles. Corey no longer cares at all. He just wants to get this whole ordeal over with. Corey no longer feels fear. How could it be any worse than what he had already endured? What he feels is more like anxiety. He rocks back and forth with his chin resting gently on his knees as his arms neatly secured his body into a tight ball. It is now approaching 2:00 a.m. Time to go! Corey reluctantly nudges Jarvis, his elbow lightly pressing into Jarvis' side. He hates to do it. Jarvis is in a very deep sleep, even snoring. Corey pushes a bit harder the second time around and whispers, "Come on Jay; it's time to get up!" Jarvis is disoriented as he tries to open his eyes but just ends up steadily blinking to gain consciousness of what is going on. Jarvis finally turns onto his back and groans, in a low raspy voice, "What's up?" to Corey, his eyes squinted. "Come on Jay. It's time. We gotta go, now!" Jarvis disappointedly asks Corey, "Why exactly are we doing this again? I'm tired dude. Can we do this tomorrow?" Corey firmly replies, "No, get the fuck up now, Jay before someone catches us. I told you before. We ain't safe here; let's go!" Corey is profoundly aware of the danger they are in understanding that a drunk Dan is probably ten times worse than a sober Dan. The last they saw of Dan, his kids were assisting him into bed with Mary, who didn't seem enthused about his condition. Corey knows this is their only shot, and they need to act fast. "Just grab what you can. We will worry about the rest later. I will find a way to get Sarah to bring us what we left." Jarvis rolls his eyes as he starts gathering some clothes and a pair of shoes to wear and one to stuff into his bookbag. Jarvis is done dressing and has his bookbag on his shoulders. Corey tiptoes to the door connected to the hallway and slowly cracks it open. He looks left down the hall then right; the coast appears clear as he waves Jarvis to follow him. They both painstakingly take each step not to even stir a creak in the floor. What would've normally taken thirty seconds, must've taken them ten minutes, going from the bedroom to the back door and onto the patio. Corey carefully closes the sliding glass door, takes a deep breath, and turns towards the night. There is no turning back now. They start to run towards the street. Off into the darkness they go.

Corey and Jarvis briskly walk in the blackness of the Beaumont Estates while trying to get their directional bearings together. Jarvis, perplexed, asks Corey, "I thought you knew the way to the Mini-Mart we saw the other day; you said it wasn't that far from here." Exasperated, Corey responds, "I do, or I did. But it's dark now, and I can't make out the streets as well. Trust me, though. I think we're headed in the right direction." Jarvis starts to get irate. "You keep asking me to trust you, and I don't even know what the hell is going on. I could be in bed resting, then waking up to a huge Sunday breakfast and probably chilling all day because Dan is too wasted to have us slaving around. But no, I'm out here in the middle of the night, and we don't know where we are or where we're going. I'm pissed right now," yells Jarvis into the night sky. The old Corey would have gotten his feelings hurt by Jarvis' statements and possibly suggested turning back But the new Corey stops, grabs Jarvis by the neck, and throws him to the ground. Corey holds his elbow against Jarvis' neck firmly as he says, "Look, this is the last fucking time I'm going to explain this to you. Dan is a very dangerous man, and you're too stupid to see it, but I do. I'm trying my best to protect you, to protect us. I don't have time to explain it right now; we gotta get to the store and call Macho. I promise I will explain everything once we're safe, but for now, we need to stay focused!" Corey removes his elbow and helps Jarvis off the ground. Jarvis, holding his throat as if he is injured, seems stunned by Corey's aggression but quietly dusts himself off and continues to follow Corey into the night. Even at this time of the morning, there is still an occasional firework blast or gun shot in the distance, normal sounds for a lively 4th of July holiday. The boys trudge on as despair and fatigue starts to set in, though they have only been traveling for about thirty minutes. The mental anguish of uncertainty is what weighs them down. Suddenly, Corey stops, "I recognize this. I remember this from the other day; the store should be about three blocks away." Corey gets a jolt of energy and starts to run in the direction of where his memory tells him the store should be. Jarvis, without uttering a word, starts to run as well. They both continue to sprint for about eight minutes nonstop, and then, there it is. The Mini-Mart is in the exact spot that Corey predicted that it would be. The store is closed, but there is a light illuminating the parking lot. The boys lay down on the sidewalk, mentally and physically exhausted.

They rest there for a couple of minutes to catch their breath. Then Corey riffles through his pockets and retrieves some loose change and the crumpled piece of paper with Macho's number on it. Jarvis quietly remains seated on the sidewalk while Corey goes to place the phone call to Macho. Corey picks up the phone, puts a quarter in the slot, and carefully dials all seven digits on the paper. He patiently leans against the phone booth as he awaits someone to answer his call. The phone rings and rings and without an answer. Corey is hunched over trying to remain calm but growing increasingly stressed with each ring. Figuring he may have misdialed the number, he goes to hang up and redial when he hears a faint voice say, "Hello." So shocked, he drops the phone, which narrowly misses the ground if not for the cord. Corey grabs the phone and holds it up to his ear and replies, "Hello, is Macho there? Could I please talk to him?" He speaks in a timid tone to the person on the other line. After a long period of silence, the person on the other end replies, "Who is this and why are calling my house at this hour?" a woman's voice angrily pierces through the phone. Corey sheepishly replies, "I am so sorry to call your house at this hour ma'am, honestly, but this is very important. If you could please give him the phone, it would mean so much. Thank you." Again, there is another long pause without even a peep, then a loud sigh and the "clank" sound of the phone being laid down. Corey breathes his own sigh of relief as he hopes she is going to give Macho the phone. Corey waits for what seems like an eternity. Jarvis breaks his silent treatment to eagerly ask Corey what is going on, and what did Macho say? Corey holds his hand over the mouthpiece of the phone and whispers, "I'm still waiting for him to get to the phone. Someone is getting him now, I think." Jarvis nods as if to accept the answer, but his body language and facial expression display annoyance at the entire situation. Corey observes Jarvis' skepticism but ignores it as he still very much believes that they are in imminent danger. Corey is again resisting the urge to hang up since he has waited so long for someone to come back to the phone. Dejected, his head hangs low in defeat. As the time passes, Corey's brain begins to wonder, what is plan B? He hadn't even thought that far. Maybe see if Jarvis has enough money to take a cab to their apartment complex, though Corey knows Jarvis doesn't have any money, nor does he. He could call his parents to come get them, but that would be disastrous as it would surely end in them abusing him for waking them up. Corey feels hopeless, and he listens to the faint sound of a TV on the other end of the phone. He is about to concede and just tell Jarvis they can start walking back to the Butler's house and figure out the next move by afternoon when he finally hears a crumpling noise coming from the earpiece. Corey listens intensively as he waits for a voice to come through the line. Finally, a crackly, deep voice speaks, "Who is this? It better be good calling at 3:00 a.m." Corey responds with delight, "Macho, is that you? This is Corey, from Coach Dan's house." "Oh, hey man, Yeah, it's Macho. What's up? You okay?" Macho's demeanor relaxes once he realizes out who it is. Corey explains, "No, we're not okay; we're in danger. We left the coach's house just now because Dan has been drinking tonight, and he also made some threats to me. Man, it was just time to go." "Where y'all at?" asks Macho, who sounds genuinely concerned. "We're at the Mini-Mart on Harrison Avenue. Do you think you can come get us now? We just need to get away from this area all together. Maybe lay low at your house until Jarvis' mom gets back in town tomorrow, if that's okay with you," Corey pleads with Macho for his help. Macho's response puts Corey at ease, "No problem. I know exactly where that is. Let me get dressed, and I should be there in less than twenty minutes. Y'all hold tight." Corey breathes a big sigh of relief. "Awe man, thanks a million. We will be right here waiting by the payphone; see you in a bit." Corey hangs up, claps his hands, and yells, "YES!" Jarvis just rolls his eyes, still in the dark about what is truly going on. Corey plops down beside Jarvis, throws his arm around his neck, and says, "We're gonna be okay, Jay; this is all going to work out. Macho will be here soon to get us." Jarvis reluctantly gives Corey a little grin, then says, "That's good, but could you please fill me in about what the hell is going on once this is all over?" Corey replies enthusiastically, "Absolutely!" Jarvis says, "Cool, let's get a nap before Macho gets here. I'm tired as hell." Corey agrees, and they both arrange their bags comfortably on the cement to act as pillows so they can get some rest.

The boys are abruptly awakened by a car entering the parking lot of the Mini-Mart. Before Jarvis can get his bearings, the car door slams, and Corey realizes that it is Dan who has pulled into the parking lot and not Macho. "Oh shit," Corey mumbles to himself. Corey leans over to shake Jarvis, "Wake up. Dan just pulled up." Before Jarvis can react, Dan grabs Corey by the collar and punches him in the face as hard as he can while he is still on the ground. The punch is so savage, it causes Corey's head to hit the concrete and his blood to splatter all over Jarvis. "I'm gonna kill you nigger," yells Dan as he proceeds to pummel Corey, who is limp from the initial punch and not even defending himself. By now, Jarvis has come to his senses and rushes Dan to stop him from brutalizing Corey any further. Jarvis knocks Dan to the ground and the two roll around aggressively, each trying to assert dominance. After tussling for about thirty seconds, Jarvis gets the upper hand and has Dan pinned down with his knees. He swings wildly and connects on just about every punch to Dan's face and shoulders. While all of this is taking place, Corey is injured and unable to help Jarvis. He is unaware of what is going on, as he lies motionless on the ground. Jarvis is holding his own and has Dan handily subdued when it becomes simultaneously apparent to him that Dan isn't really moving anymore, and Corey is gravely injured. He instantly makes the decision to shift his focus from beating Dan to death to helping his friend. He gets off Dan's motionless body and runs over to Corey. Jarvis kneels beside Corey, who is bleeding from the mouth and nose. "Yo Corey, you gonna be okay. You were right; Dan is a psycho." Corey must've temporarily lost consciousness after Dan attacked him. He is somewhat coherent while Jarvis is talking to him but gurgling as he struggles to get words out. Jarvis instructs Corey not to talk but informs him that he is about to call 9-1-1 so help can come. Jarvis hops up and is about to run to the payphone, when Dan goes to hit him in the head with the butt end of the gun that he was showing off earlier at the barbecue. He misses his head but catches him in his right shoulder blade. Jarvis is startled by this; he didn't realize that Dan was no longer lying in the spot he last saw him. The blow cripples Jarvis as he falls to the ground in agonizing pain. Dan had used what little strength he had left to bludgeon Jarvis.

After the blow, Dan also falls to the ground, in pain and exhausted. Now all three are lying in the parking lot, wounded. Jarvis knows he cannot remain there; he must get to that phone to call the police. Jarvis thrusts himself on to his feet, making sure he doesn't put any pressure on his arm or shoulder, which he believes is broken or dislocated. As soon as he is up on his feet, Dan reaches out and grabs Jarvis by the leg. This causes Jarvis to fall directly onto the arm he is trying to protect. Jarvis hears a loud "cracking" sound as he hits the concrete with force. He screams so loudly that every home on that block probably heard him cry out.

Hearing Jarvis yell like this causes Corey to come out of his foggy state. He shakes his head and blinks a couple of times, but his vision is still blurry. He can just barely make out Jarvis, who is laying just a few feet in front of him, rolling on the ground and whimpering. He then glances to his left, where he sees what appears to be Dan. With every blink, his vision becomes clearer. Corey sees Dan reach for something lying beside him. One more blink, and as clear as day, he realizes that Dan has a gun in his hand and is trying to aim it at Jarvis. Corey musters up every bit of strength that he has and thrusts himself in Dan's direction. Then "BOOM!" It is the loud, echoing sound of Dan's gun discharging a shot into the night. The noise startles Jarvis, who believes that he must be hit. He glances to see Dan and Corey lying in the parking lot. There is a lot of blood, so it is hard to tell if anyone is injured from the gunshot. Just as Jarvis starts to drag himself over to Corey, Macho screeches into the parking lot. Jarvis can also make out a few people in the background running over to see what is going on. Once Jarvis sees all these people, he collapses in exhaustion, believing that he should now be safe. Jarvis starts to slip in and out of consciousness as the pain from his injury overwhelms him. The last thing he hazily sees before blacking out is Macho viciously stomping Dan in the back and head then kicking the gun away from him. He also thinks he sees Mary, Sarah, and Michael standing in the distance, watching the grizzly scene. But then again, this could all be a dream. Maybe he and Corey are still asleep on their bookbags waiting for Macho to come get them and none of this is really happening. Jarvis can hear the faint sound of sirens and people asking if he is okay. It all seems to be happening in slow motion. He whispers, "I just want to get some sleep." Jarvis could no longer hold his heavy eyelids open. Suddenly, the whole scene turned into complete blackness.

Jarvis opens his eyes slightly to a very blurry scene. He blinks his squinted eyes and recognizes his mom, his dad, and a white lady with a white outfit on. Jarvis thinks he is dreaming again and calls out to his mother. "Mommy." His voice so weak, it could barely be heard over the machines he is connected to. Nae immediately runs to Jarvis' bedside. "Yes baby, you're awake. Thank you, Lord." Nae, who is very religious, began to cry out and thank God that her only baby is awake and going to be okay. Jarvis is confused by the entire scene. The fact that both of his parents are there together really baffles him. And to make matters more perplexing, he sees Rick pop up from a chair in the corner of the room. It's Rick's face, but his hair is neat. He is dressed in business casual clothes, and he has on a police badge. Jarvis is really starting to think this is some weird dream now. Jarvis' dad just smiles at him as he grabs his hand, and his eyes look watery. He seems overcome with emotion which makes it hard for him to speak at that moment. Rick leans in close and waves, "Hey buddy. Good to see you awake. Once you eat and feel better, we're going to talk soon. I know you must be confused right now.

There's a lot I need to go over with you, but for now, get some rest." Jarvis nods and is shocked to hear his mom say, "Thank you Detective Clarke." His whole mind is blown when he discovers that Rick is actually a detective.

This is just getting stranger by the second. With everything that is going on in the room, Jarvis hadn't noticed that his arm and shoulder are bandaged in a hard cast until he goes to motion as if he is going to get up from his bed. Everyone in the room begins to yell, "No, no, don't move." This is when Jarvis realizes that he is in the hospital. It is all beginning to make sense now. Everything that happened at the Mini-Mart was true, and it wasn't a dream. Jarvis closes his eyes and began to play it all back in his head. After a few seconds, Jarvis immediately opens his eyes wide and shouts out, "Where's Corey? Is my friend okay? Where is he?" Everyone in the room goes to calm Jarvis down, as he again tries to get up from his hospital bed. This time, Jarvis stops himself due to the extreme pain his overexertion has caused. He winces at the throbbing discomfort and readjusts himself back into the spot he was in originally. Out of breath, Jarvis calmly asks the entire room, "Where is Corey?" Nae steps forward and places her hand on Jarvis' face. "Baby, Corey is in the ICU; he was shot by Dan. He's on the third floor, room 314. We are hoping he pulls through, but he is alive baby. And you're alive because of him. He saved you Jarvis." Nae begins to cry as she explains to Jarvis what Corey did for him. Jarvis tries to hold back his emotions but tears stream down his face as he learns the truth of what really happened that morning at the Mini-Mart. "Can I see him?" Jarvis asks in a dispirited tone. By now, there isn't a dry eye in the room. The nurse on duty speaks up, "I will check in with the ICU to see if he can have visitors." Other than the sound of sniffling and the machines, there is a dead silence in the room. Then Nae finally speaks, "Well, baby, we're going to let you eat dinner, get your meds, a bath, and I think they are going to take your catheter out. We will be in the hallway waiting. Just yell if you need us." Devastated by all the information he has just received; Jarvis looks stoically at the ceiling. While exiting the hospital room, Jarvis overhears Rick telling his parents not to talk to the news crews in the lobby, and that this story is now in the national headlines. The heavy wood door closes behind them.

Two days have passed since Jarvis learned that Corey was shot by Dan. He has been anxiously asking all the nurses, doctors, and even Rick, whose real name is Andre, if he can see Corey. Finally, the news that Jarvis has been impetuously waiting for. Corey has successfully recovered from surgery, his vitals are stable, and he should be able to have visitors later in the evening. Jarvis can hardly contain his excitement about the news. He will finally get to see the person who saved his life. He asks his mom to get a present from the gift shop so he could give it to Corey during his visit. The media outlets have been clamoring for an interview with Jarvis. They are even offering him compensation to be present for their first meeting since the "Mini-Mart Melee," which is what the national news are calling the incident. Jarvis has continually turned them down and wants to have a private meeting with Corey before he consents to any interviews. However, Jarvis has met with detective Andre Clarke on several occasions. During these interactions, Jarvis learned about all the abuse allegations that Dan had been accused of for years. He also became aware that Macho is the reason that the investigation started to gain traction.

Andre was placed in Heritage Park to start the investigation back in 1983 following an anonymous tip by a concerned citizen. Andre informs Jarvis that he believes the mysterious citizen was Mary Butler, but that has never been verified. He told Jarvis that he would have had this case wrapped up years ago if any of the boys had just come forward. But none of them ever wanted to talk. Andre tells Jarvis of his frustrations trying so hard to create a safe and comfortable environment for nonjudgmental dialogue. But the boys that he knew had stayed at Dan's house all of those summers were too scared to talk. He knew that he had an uphill battle given Dan's prominence in the community. But he was astonished at how deep the code of silence that existed within the Black community was. Macho was the first kid to open up and talk about his experience at Dan's house. He was terrified, ashamed, and somehow, felt that it was his fault. Technically, Macho was ordered not to get involved with the investigation under any circumstances. But he was so concerned about the safety of the boys that he saw in Dan's yard that day, he couldn't help it. And looking back, thank God that he interceded that fateful day. Deep down inside, Jarvis wonders what happened to Dan, but at the end of the day, it doesn't matter. Rick has assured him that he will never have to worry about Dan again for as long as he lives. He was detained shortly after the boys were taken to the hospital. But not before Macho got some retribution for the injustices Dan had with him years earlier. Jarvis has gone over and over in his mind many times how Corey saved him from Dan. Not just the Mini-Mart incident, but all those times at Dan's house, Corey interjected and put himself in harm's way for the sake of their friendship. Jarvis is experiencing severe feelings of guilt because of the whole situation. There's that whole thing with Corey's mom that had been eating him up for months. But the fact that hurts Jarvis the most is if it weren't for him, Corey would not have even been at Dan's house that summer. Jarvis has met with a staff therapist and will have ongoing treatment for a very long time. But he feels that once he sees Corey, it could relax his tortured mind just a bit.

There is a soft knock on the door of room 314. A weak, raspy voice answers from the inside, "Come in." Jarvis pops his head in and gives a big warm smile to Corey, who has been anxiously awaiting Jarvis' arrival. "What up boy?" Jarvis affectionately addresses his good friend. "Hey Jay," Corey tries his best to mirror Jarvis' enthusiasm, but he is in excruciating pain. Jarvis invites himself into the hospital room and sits down in a chair directly beside Corey's bed. Jarvis sets the gift he has down on the floor beside him. Jarvis is trying his best to remain upbeat and not react to the horrific condition Corey is in, but he is stunned at what he is facing. Corey's entire head is bandaged, revealing nothing but his eyes and face. His lips are swollen, and he has several teeth missing. There is also a dressing on Corey's abdomen, covering the gunshot wound he endured. The constant beeping of the numerous machines and IVs hooked to his frail body are overwhelming to Jarvis, but he does not react. Jarvis gently asks Corey if he feels like talking, and Corey nods. Jarvis assures Corey that he would do most of the talking so that he can preserve his energy.

Jarvis starts out by asking Corey, "Your folks come by to see you yet?" Corey nods. "That's good," Jarvis replies. "You eat yet?" Jarvis nervously continues his small talk. Corey nods again, then jokingly jeers, "Stop being weird nigga." Jarvis bursts out laughing at Corey's unexpected sense of humor under the circumstances. Corey initially laughs with Jarvis but immediately regrets it. He ends up in excruciating pain at the sight of his stomach wound. Jarvis desperately apologizes and asks if he should call the nurse. Corey assures Jarvis he is fine as he gives the "thumbs down." Jarvis breathes a sigh of relief that his friend is still in good spirits. Jarvis' demeanor suddenly becomes somber, "Look, I don't want to get all mushy, but I don't know how else to say this. So, I'm just gonna come right out with it. Thank you for being such a good friend, Corey. Thank you for saving my life. Thank you for trying to warn me about that lunatic so many times. I am so sorry I didn't listen to you sooner. I am so sorry I got you into this situation. It's completely my fault, and I will spend the rest of my life trying to repay you. I only hope," Jarvis starts to break down in the middle of his outpouring. Tears erupt from his eyes as he hangs his head in shame. Mainly because of the role he played in everything that has taken place. He is also embarrassed by his crying so intensely in front of Corey. Jarvis takes a deep breath, clears his throat, and attempts to finish his thoughts. "I only hope that you can find a way to forgive me." Corey does not react initially. They sit for some time in tranquility. Only the sound of the machines can be heard.

The silence is deafening and concerns Jarvis. It causes him to clinch Corey's hands while he drops his head in despair. Jarvis quietly begins to cry again when Corey feebly reacts to his gush of raw emotion. "Jay, you know you my man. I would do it all again if I could. Truth is, I always wanted to be like you. Strong, fast, smart. All the girls like you, and you dress good. Your parents give a damn about you. It made me want to protect you. Dudes like you don't hang out with dudes like me, yet you are always there for me. I did it because of all you have done for me Jay. You are my only friend. If you had any idea of the shit I been through in my life, then you would understand how much just having one friend really means. Not to sound like a fag, but I love you Jay, and whether you know it or not, you saved my life first." Jarvis is inconsolable as he leans in and gives Corey a delicate hug, so he doesn't hurt his wounds. Jarvis is fighting the urge to tell Corey about his situation with his mom. Jarvis is about to come clean and confront his guilty conscious as he starts, "Look Corey, I have something else to te–" Corey interrupts Jarvis' thought, "I hate to cut you off Jay, but I'm so tired right now. All this sissy shit has me exhausted." Jarvis grins, still amazed at how lighthearted Corey is. "We can talk some more tomorrow if you want," Corey yawns for effect to show how tired he is. Jarvis can sense that Corey is faking. He is starting to wonder if Corey knows more than he is letting on. It seems like he intentionally finds a way to avoid this very conversation every time it comes up. Jarvis agrees to let his friend get some rest and promises to pop back in tomorrow. Jarvis feels so much better after talking to his best friend. He turns to walk out into the hallway and suddenly remembers that he hadn't given Corey the gift he had for him. Just as Jarvis turns to retrieve the gift and present it to Corey quickly before he leaves, the machines he is hooked to start to seamlessly blare. The noise startles Jarvis and before he can react to it, a wave of doctors and nurses rush into the room, pushing him out of the way. Jarvis finds himself trying to peer over the heads of medical professionals that have filled the small space. He can't make out what the jumbled voices are saying. One word is loud and clear, "flatline." Jarvis tries to fight his way through the crowd so he can get to his friend. He suddenly feels someone grab his waist and pull him into the cold hallway. The door to room 314 slams in Jarvis' face as the doctors work feverishly to revive Corey.

The End

Do you think Dan is the only villain in this book? How many people do you think let Corey and Jarvis down throughout this story? Do you consider Dan a victim? Should there be a follow-up to this manuscript? Your thoughts and input are valuable to me. Please let me know any feedback that you may have, good or bad on one of the platforms listed below. Thanks, and I hope that you enjoyed this story!

RVAauthorbae: Instagram

RVAauthorbae@gmail.com

If you, or anyone that you know is the victim of any form of abuse, please get help! Below is the name of a licensed professional who specializes in trauma and abuse therapy.

Latisha S. Christensen, MSW, LCSW-QS, LISW-CP, LCSW-C, BC-TMH

Specialties: Trauma, Finance, Narcissistic Abuse Survivors & Race Relations

latishachristensen@gmail.com

410-670-5889/813-358-2268

www.ingramcontent.com/pod-product-compliance
Lightning Source LLC
Chambersburg PA
CBHW070823250626
47170CB00006B/2198